ON MY TERMS

ASHLEY FARLEY

ALSO BY ASHLEY FARLEY

Palmetto Island

Muddy Bottom

Change of Tides

Lowcountry on My Mind

Sail Away

Hope Springs Series

Dream Big, Stella!

Show Me the Way

Mistletoe and Wedding Bells

Matters of the Heart

Stand Alone

Tangled in Ivy

Lies that Bind

Life on Loan

Only One Life

Home for Wounded Hearts

Nell and Lady

Sweet Tea Tuesdays

Saving Ben

Sweeney Sisters Series

Saturdays at Sweeney's

Tangle of Strings

Boots and Bedlam

Lowcountry Stranger

Her Sister's Shoes

Magnolia Series

Beyond the Garden

Magnolia Nights

Scottie's Adventures

Breaking the Story

Merry Mary

THE SETUP

Rain pounds the roof of my parked car as I watch for activity at the two-story brick home across the street. A bolt of lightning brightens the night sky, illuminating the other stately homes on the block. Headlights approach from the rear, and a black Chevrolet Suburban stops alongside the curb in front of the house. The interior lights come on inside the SUV as the occupants—a man and woman—emerge from the other side. When the Uber takes off again, I raise my compact binoculars and follow the couple as they sprint, with raincoat hoods pulled tight over their heads, up the short sidewalk to the front porch. The man's gait is oddly familiar. How many people own orange raincoats? I dismiss the idea. Too much of a coincidence.

I focus the binoculars on the woman. When she reaches the porch, she peels off her drenched raincoat. I recognize her from social media pics as Nora Riley, the subject of my investigation. She walks into the man's outstretched arms. He too has shed his raincoat, and I can now see his face. My breath hitches. So it *is* the rotten bastard.

I wait for the couple to enter the house. Tugging a black cap over my head, I stuff my camera inside my raincoat and dash across the street. I duck down in the shrubs in front of the porch while I catch my breath. Holding the camera up to protect it, I slither on my belly across the wooden floor and peer in the window. Through the dining room, I can see into the wide center hallway where the couple is tearing at each other's clothes. The sight of my husband's hand on Nora's firm ass makes my blood boil. I stand suddenly, but the lovers are too preoccupied to notice movement in the window. Slinging the camera strap around my neck, I remove my handgun from its holster on my hip. With gun aimed at the ceiling, I creep along the front of the house to where the sounds of lustful groans drift through the open front door.

Stepping over the threshold into the house, I extend my arms in front of me and aim the gun at my husband's head. My finger is on the trigger, and I'm preparing to shoot, when it dawns on me that I've been set up. And Lucas is definitely not worth going to jail for. I lower and uncock the gun, sliding it back in its holster. The lovers have dropped to the floor, and Nora is riding my husband like a cowgirl at a rodeo with blonde hair dancing about her shoulders and fake breasts bouncing around like water balloons. I focus the camera lens and press the shutter, holding it down while the camera records dozens of images of their exposed bodies and faces.

Spinning on my heels, I dart across the porch and run, blinded by tears, back down the sidewalk. When I near the end, I slip on the wet bluestone and stumble into the front yard. Righting myself, I traipse through the sodden grass to the street and cross the pavement to my car.

I speed through the streets of Richmond's Fan District to the dumpy apartment where Lucas and I live. Blissfully in love, I was more than willing to move into his bachelor pad after our spontaneous wedding three years ago. I assumed we would spruce up the place, make it feel more like a home. But Lucas refused to let me paint the dingy tan walls, let alone buy new furniture.

In the spare bedroom we use as a home office, I open my laptop and insert the memory card from my camera. Images of the naked lovers fill the screen of my photo editor. I download the files onto a thumb drive and eject the memory card. I spend a few minutes editing the most revealing of the images, adjusting the highlights and shadows before printing two copies. Pocketing the memory card, I place one of the copies in a backpack with my laptop and camera and the other on Lucas's pillow in our bedroom.

I fold my hanging clothes into my rolling suitcase and empty my drawers into a duffel bag. When I go into the bathroom for my toiletries, I catch sight of myself in the mirror. My hair hangs in damp strands around my face, and mascara runs in rivulets down my cheeks. No wonder Lucas cheated on me. I can't compete with glamorous socialites like Nora Riley.

My mind travels back decades to another life. I still remember the haunted look in my mother's blue eyes, so like the pair staring out of the mirror at me now, when she abandoned my brother and me in front of the police department in Amarillo, Texas. I still remember her words. "I'm sorry it's come to this. But I never wanted to be a mother."

I gather my toiletries into a cosmetic case, toss the case into the duffel, and place both bags beside the door. I circle the living room one last time, pausing to stare out of the sliding glass door. Weeds grow through cracks in the brick patio, and the annuals I planted in containers have long since wilted under the summer sun. The hood stands open on the rusty gas grill revealing charred chicken breasts on the grates. The burnt dinner had been the source of our most recent argument. So what if I'm not a gourmet cook? At least I try. Lucas's idea of an evening at home consists of drinking beer, playing video games, and ordering delivery takeout.

Turning away from the window, I leave the apartment without looking back. I store my luggage in the trunk of my car and drive to the heart of downtown and enter a parking garage. Despite the late hour, men and women in professional attire come and go from the marble and glass lobby. Taking the elevator to the fifth floor, I pass through the law firm's vacant reception area and walk down the long hallway until I find the man I'm looking for in the corner office. Laurence Riley is working at his ginormous mahogany desk, an antique banker's lamp spilling light onto the document he's studying. Riley appears older in person than he sounded on the phone, but he's a strikingly handsome man with strong facial features and thick dark hair graying at the temples.

I clear my throat before entering his office. Riley looks up, tosses his pen on the desk, and sits back in his chair. "How'd it go? Did you accomplish your mission?"

I jab a finger at him. "You set me up. You knew your wife was sleeping with my husband. That's why you hired me instead of one of those high-dollar investigators your firm keeps on retainer. Were you hoping I'd go ballistic and kill them?"

His lip curls in a smug smile as he eyes the holstered weapon on my hip. "Well? Did you?"

I glare at him. "I'm not a murderer. When I left your house, our spouses were alive and screwing their brains out." I drop the photograph and one of the thumb drives on his desk, and hold out my hand. "I want my money."

He opens his top desk drawer and removes a wad of twenties. "It's all there. I trust you can see yourself out."

I turn my back on him and storm out of his office. Returning to my car, I drive three blocks to the high-rise waterfront condominium building where my twin brother lives. I drag my luggage through the lobby and take the elevator to the eighth floor. I pound on Jason's door until he answers. He's still wearing scrubs, and his sandy hair is sticking up on one side.

I experience a pang of guilt. Sleep is a precious commodity for him. "Did I wake you?"

"Long day. I fell asleep on the sofa reading a medical journal."

Despite being fraternal twins, we look nothing alike. I'm the washed-out version. His hair is golden. Mine is the color of wheat. His eyes are a dazzling blue. Mine are pale and dull.

His gaze travels to the suitcases at my feet. "Please tell me you finally left that prick."

With a solemn nod, I say, "I caught him cheating on me. Can I crash with you for a few days?"

"Stay as long as you like. But take the shoes off first."

I stare down at my mud-crusted running shoes. "Oops."

"Have you been mud wrestling again, Jolie?"

"Aren't you the comedian?" I kick off my shoes. "There."

"Now you may enter." Jason grabs my duffel bag and steps out of the way.

My brother's apartment is spotless and sparsely furnished. He's an anesthesiologist resident who spends most of his time at the hospital. He has few needs outside of sleep and nourishment.

I wheel my suitcase behind him down a short hallway to the guest room. Jason tosses my duffel onto the queen-size bed and turns on the lamp on the nightstand. "Sheets are clean. Make yourself at home. Have you eaten dinner yet?"

I set my suitcase upright beside the door. "I'm not hungry, but I could use a drink. Do you have any tequila?"

He gives me a that's-a-dumb-question look. He can't stand the stuff, but he keeps a bottle of tequila on hand for my infrequent visits.

We return to the living room. I take a seat at the island in the adjacent kitchen, watching Jason as he drops a single large cube of ice in a glass and covers the cube with tequila.

He slides the glass across the granite. "What happened with Lucas?"

"He's sleeping with some rich lawyer's wife." I take a gulp of tequila before walking him through the night's events.

He listens intently, leaning against the counter with arms crossed. He waits for me to finish talking before asking, "Since when did you become a private investigator?"

I shrug. "It pays the bills."

"What about your journalist gig?"

"There is no gig. I wrote a few freelance pieces. But none of the news outlets were interested in buying them."

"And your podcast?"

Holding up three fingers, I say, "I have three subscribers. You being one of them. The other two are random people who wanted follow backs."

"You're better than this, Jolie. Why settle for less than you deserve?" He comes around the island and sits down next to me. "You put me through medical school. Now it's my turn to support you. Why don't you go to college and get a degree?"

Planting my elbows on the counter, I stare down at my drink. "A degree in what?"

"Journalism. Duh."

"I'm taking online writing and photography classes. My skills are improving. These things take time." I run my finger around the rim of my glass. "I'm not like you, Jason. You're the student. I'm more of a boots-on-the-ground kinda girl."

"You could always return to the police force."

"Maybe. I'll figure out my career later. First, I need to get out of this marriage. Do you know a good divorce attorney?"

"I do, actually." Jason thumbs through the contacts on his

phone. "Chris is young. He doesn't have much experience, but he's a real hard ass. He won't take any crap from Lucas."

Jason shares the contact and seconds later my phone pings with the incoming message. "At least I succeeded at one thing," I say.

He looks up from his phone. "What's that?"

"I broke the record for short marriages."

Jason nudges me with his elbow. "Come on, Jolie! Plenty of people have shorter marriages."

"Name one."

He pauses before answering. "I can't. I don't know that many married people." He shrugs. "You made a mistake by getting married too young."

I drain the rest of the tequila. "You tried to tell me. I should've listened to you."

"I'm certainly not an authority on matters of the heart. I've never even had a serious girlfriend."

I let out a grunt. "Whose fault is that? You always have plenty of girls chasing you."

"My schedule doesn't allow much free time for dating. Besides, relationships are complicated."

"Don't I know it." I rest my head on his shoulder. "You need a wife, bro, a loving woman who will support your career and give you beautiful babies."

"Maybe one day. I'd like to offer a child the loving home we never had." He drapes his arm around my shoulders. "Don't worry, sis. You'll find the right man, and when the time is right, you'll make an excellent mother."

"No way am I bringing an innocent child into this screwed-up world."

Jason gets to his feet and holds out his hand to me. "You say that now. You'll feel better about things after you've had a good night's sleep."

I'M TOO restless to sleep. Every time I close my eyes, I see Nora and Jason's naked bodies. After an hour of staring at the ceiling, I get out of bed and rummage through my suitcase for my favorite pair of faded jeans. I button on a loose-fitting black blouse and step into my cowboy boots. In the adjoining bathroom, I splash cold water on my face, touch up my makeup, and brush the knots out of my hair.

Tiptoeing past Jason's bedroom, I let myself out of the apartment and take an Uber to my favorite watering hole. Carrigan's is usually packed with young professionals on Wednesday nights. But the weather has kept everyone at home. I sit down at the end of the bar and wait for Drew to notice me.

Drew has a warm and fuzzy effect on me. He's one of the good guys. He has a huge heart to go with his innocent baby face and angelic blond curls.

About a year ago, after a particularly nasty argument with Lucas, I fled our apartment in a blind rage and landed here where I drank straight tequila while pouring my heart out to Drew. He's a good listener. Although I've noticed he pays me more attention than his other customers. He has a crush on me, which he doesn't bother to hide. He gives me drinks on the house and tells me I look pretty. I've tried not to lead him on. I've told him I was committed to making my marriage work. But that marriage is now over. I've often fantasized about sleeping with Drew. Now there's nothing stopping me.

Drew finishes with a customer and makes his way toward me. "Hey, gorgeous. What can I get you? The usual?"

"Please. And make it a double."

"Uh-oh." He slides a paper cocktail napkin in front of me. "Trouble in Paradise?"

I shake my head. "You have no idea."

"Hold that thought." He makes my drink and places it on the cocktail napkin. "We'll be closing soon. Better guzzle that if you plan to have another." He drops his elbows to the bar. "Talk to me. What's going on?"

"I caught Lucas with another woman. Our marriage is over. End of story."

"I'm sorry, Jolie. You deserve better than that." Drew straightens. "But you can't drop a bombshell like that without giving me the details."

I pause a beat while I argue with my conscience. I'm obligated to keep my client's identity private. Then again, Riley set me up. I owe him nothing.

I nurse my drink while I repeat the story for the second time.

When I'm finished, Drew brings the bottle over and pours another splash of tequila in my glass. "I don't know what to say, Jolie. I know how much you wanted your marriage to work."

I experience a moment of clarity. "In hindsight, I wanted it to work for the wrong reasons. Giving up on my marriage would've meant admitting defeat, admitting I made yet another colossal mistake. Lucky me, I get to add divorce to my long list of failures. My brother is the rock star. I'm the black sheep of the family."

"I don't believe that."

"It's true." If only Drew knew the half of it.

I sit back in my chair, noticing the last of the customers have left the restaurant. "Do you need to lock up?"

"Yes. But we don't have to leave just yet." He pours himself a draft beer, and comes from behind the bar, locking the front door and sitting down next to me.

"You know, I actually feel an enormous sense of relief." I hold my shoulders back and head high. "I'm finally rid of the ten-ton weight I've been dragging around for three years. Good riddance, Lucas." I punch the air. "I'm free."

The song currently playing on the sound system ends, and

"Dancing in the Moonlight" comes on. I down the rest of my tequila. "I love this song. Let's dance." Before he can object, I slide off the barstool and drag him onto the dance floor.

"This is seriously cool," I yell above the music. "I've never had a bar all to myself before."

"I agree," he says, giving me a thumbs-up. "I like being here alone late at night."

The song ends, and a slow one begins. Hooking an arm around my waist, he pulls me close. He's only a few inches taller than me, and my body fits perfectly against his. Resting my head on his broad chest, we shuffle from side to side. I feel his excitement against my thigh, and when I look up at him, he brushes his lips against mine. I kiss him back. Our lips part and tongues meet. He walks me backward, pinning me against the wall. His hands are all over me, and my body aches for him. Being with him feels so right. All my past mistakes and hardships have brought me to this point in time. Drew is my guy. We are meant to be together. I feel it in my gut, among other places. But the last thing I want to do is screw it up.

I push him away. "I can't do this."

He steps back. "You're right. Not tonight. It's too soon. I care about you, Jolie. I'm interested in more than a one-night stand."

"I—"

My Apple Watch vibrates with a notification from a local news network. The headline reads: HOMICIDE AT HOME OF LOCAL ATTORNEY.

I wave my phone at the wall-mounted television behind the bar. "Quick! Turn on the TV."

Drew retrieves the remote and powers on the TV, tuning to the local news station. A journalist, her dark hair matted from drizzle, is standing on the sidewalk in front of the Riley house where yellow crime scene tape outlines the perimeter of the property. According to the reporter, city police were called to the scene after the homeowner, prominent area criminal attorney Laurence Riley, arrived home to find his wife shot to death by an intruder.

His wife? What about Lucas?

"What's going on, Jolie? Do you know these people?"

My eyes remained glued to the television. "I was at that house earlier. My husband was sleeping with Riley's wife!"

Drew's mouth falls open and his blue eyes get big. "Do you think your husband killed her?"

"I think it's more likely Riley killed her. Or had someone kill her for him."

The camera zooms in on Laurence Riley, who is standing on the front porch talking to police officers. Who better to plan a murder than a criminal attorney? Either Riley killed his wife, or he paid someone to do it for him. But what about Lucas? How does he fit into Riley's plan?

WRECKING BALL

The vibration of my phone on the pillow beside my head startles me out of a deep sleep. I croak out a "Morning" to my brother.

"Jolie! Are you okay? The police have been trying to reach you."

"I just woke up." Putting the phone on speaker, I scroll down the long list of missed calls from unknown numbers.

"The police need you to call them back. Any clue what they want?"

"I have an idea." I return the phone to my ear. "Last night, after you crashed, I couldn't sleep, so I went to Carrigan's for a nightcap. I saw a report on the news about Nora Riley's murder. I'm not sure how Lucas fits in. The journalist didn't mention him."

"But wh—"

"I can think of many possible scenarios."

Jason lets out a sigh. "The homicide detective's name is Calvin Ingram. Do you know him?"

"Never heard of him." I scramble to sit up in bed. "Did you tell him I'm staying at your apartment?"

"Nope. I told him I would try to get in touch with you."

"Good." I rake my hands through my hair. "God, my head is killing me. Do you have any Advil?"

"In my medicine cabinet," Jason says. "I'm going into surgery in a few minutes. But the procedure shouldn't take long."

"Okay. I'll text you when I have some answers."

I end the call and kick back the covers. I'm still wearing my jeans and blouse from last night. The memory of kissing Drew comes back to me. My body warms at the prospect of a future with him. But I shove the thought aside. My marriage just ended. I can't jump into another relationship until I get my head on straight.

Rolling out of bed, I stumble down the hall to Jason's bathroom and rummage in the cabinet for Advil, shaking three out of the bottle into my hand. I head for the kitchen, pour a glass of water, and down the Advil. Popping a K-cup into the Keurig machine, I watch the stream of steaming brown liquid fill my brother's Yeti mug. I take my coffee to the wall of windows and stare out at the James River flowing through downtown Richmond. The sky is hazy, heavy with humidity after last night's rain. As I sip the dark roast, I mentally replay last night's events in slow motion. Two things place me at the scene of the murder. The photos I took of Nora and Jason having sex. And my muddy tennis shoes.

What if Lucas is dead? What if Lucas killed Nora? What if Riley hired someone to kill her? So many what-ifs. I need answers.

I text Mel, an old friend in the police department. *Hey stranger. I've received several urgent messages from Detective Ingram. Any clue what he wants?*

My phone immediately rings with a call from Mel. "Jolie, it's been a long time. I'm sorry to be the one to break the news to you, but Lucas is dead."

My heart sinks. Lucas was my husband. Despite our problems and his infidelity, I never wanted him dead.

"Jolie, are you still there?"

"I'm here. How did he—"

"That's what Ingram wants to talk to you about."

I grip the phone. "Who is this Ingram person, anyway?"

"He's new to the department. He transferred in from Chicago last year. He's tough but fair. I lobbied hard for your case, but the chief considers our friendship a conflict of interest."

"So, you finally got promoted to detective. Good for you! Congrats."

"Thanks," Mel says. "I'm at the station now. Catching up on some paperwork. I can hang around if you're planning to come in. Ingram's here. I'll let him know you're on the way."

"I'll be there within the hour."

My brother has a massage head on his shower, and I stay in longer than necessary, letting the hot water beat my aching shoulders and neck while I try to wrap my mind around my husband's death.

With hair still damp, I dress in jeans and a V-neck white T-shirt. I tie my muddy running shoes in a plastic grocery bag and drop the bag in my backpack along with my card wallet and cell phone. I take the elevator to the parking deck. No one is around and most of the spaces are empty. The majority of the building's occupants are young professionals who have long since left for work.

I open my car door and toss my backpack onto the passenger's seat. I'm sliding behind the wheel when a pair of large hands jerks me to my feet. My keys fly out of my hands, dropping with a clanking noise to the pavement. My assailant's body is massive. His muscular arms are tight around my torso, his beefy paw clamped over my mouth as he wrestles me to the trunk. I squirm and kick, but my strength is no match for his. Of all the times for me to leave my weapon at home. Not that I could've gotten to it with him manhandling me this way.

He gags my mouth, zip-ties my ankles and wrists, and tosses me into the trunk. He bangs the trunk lid shut, and a minute later the car's front door slams. I hear the beeping sound of the doors locking and his rubber-soled shoes moving away from the car, not toward the street but in the opposite direction. Toward the building.

Panic overcomes me. I scream and thrash about until I'm exhausted and gasping for air. *Breathe, Jolie!* I tell myself. I inhale and exhale, as best I can with a wad of cloth in my mouth. After a long minute, my breathing steadies, the panic subsides, and my mind clears.

Think, Jolie. My phone is in my backpack in the front seat of the car. I try to get my fingers on my Apple Watch, but the zip tie cuts into my skin. I have no choice but to wait for someone to rescue me. Darkness envelops me. I close my eyes and imagine myself on a deserted beach with the waves lapping softly against the shore. I have no clue how much time passes. I drift in and out of sleep until the sound of tires screeching to a halt nearby jerks me awake.

My screams are muffled by the gag, but I don't stop yelling until I hear someone prying the trunk open with a crowbar. I'm blinded by light at first, but when the little white dots clear, Mel is looming over me, lovely as ever with caramel skin and green eyes. Behind her is a man with wavy dark hair, cut close to his head, and chiseled features. His eyes are an intoxicating golden hue, the color of aged brandy.

He stands by and watches as Mel removes the gag from my mouth and cuts the zip ties from my wrists and ankles with her switchblade.

"Damn, girlfriend," Mel says. "I don't see you for years, and you come crashing back into my life like a wrecking ball. I'd forgotten how drama follows you around like a dark cloud. I'm not sure I'm ready to be your friend again."

"You don't have any choice." I extend my hand to her. "Get me outta here."

Mel hauls me out of the trunk to my feet. A wave of dizziness overcomes me, and I lean against the car until it passes.

Mel gestures at the man. "Jolie, meet Calvin Ingram. Calvin this is Jolene Hogan."

He cocks an eyebrow. "Jolene? As in the song?"

I shrug. "What can I say? My mother was a Dolly Parton fan." I don't know if this is true, but it's my standard response when someone cracks a joke about my name.

"Who did this to you?" Mel asks.

"I have no clue." I go around to the passenger side of the car and open the door. "But whoever it was stole my backpack."

Mel comes to stand beside me. "What was in the backpack?"

"My card wallet, phone, and the shoes I was wearing last night."

"Why the shoes?" Mel asks.

"It's a long story."

Calvin speaks for the first time. "I'd like to hear this story. Can we continue this party down at the station?"

"I'm not going anywhere. I just found out my husband is dead, and I spent two hours locked in a trunk. We can either have this conversation upstairs in my brother's condo, or not at all. Your choice." Without waiting for him to respond, I storm off toward the elevators.

Mel and Ingram follow me into the elevator cart, and we ride in silence to the eighth floor. When the doors open, I emerge ahead of them and start down the hall. I stop in my tracks at the sight of my brother's open door. I can see inside. Someone has ransacked his apartment.

With weapons drawn, the detectives enter the condo ahead

of me, clearing all the rooms before allowing me to enter. I survey the shambles—furniture overturned, trash littered on the kitchen floor, and clothes strewn about. Nothing appears to be missing or destroyed except my computer and camera body. Fortunately, he didn't find my gun hidden inside the air register in Jason's living room.

"Is this yours?" Mel asks, pointing at my backpack on the kitchen island.

"Yep." I reach for it, but Mel brushes my hand away.

"Don't touch it. We need to check the contents for prints."

"But my phone is in there."

Mel reaches for her radio. "I'll have a unit pick it up and take it to the station. They'll expedite it and have it back to you this afternoon."

I roll my eyes. "You won't find any prints. Whoever did this wore gloves."

Ingram restores the sofa to an upright position and motions for me to sit down. "Start talking."

I ignore him and turn to Mel. "I need some coffee. Want some?"

Mel waves me off. "I'm fine, but thanks."

Mel sits down at the island with Ingram across the room on the sofa. After I brew my coffee, I stand at the counter facing both of them. "Laurence Riley contacted me three days ago. He suspected his wife was cheating on him, and he hired me to get the dirt on her."

"How did he find out about your investigative services?" Ingram asks.

"He claims he saw my profile on LinkedIn. But he had an ulterior motive for hiring me. My husband was the one sleeping with his wife."

"Maybe it was a coincidence," Ingram says. "Maybe he didn't know your husband was the one sleeping with his wife."

"He knew. If you'll stop interrupting me, I'll tell you the whole story."

"By all means," Ingram says, settling back against the sofa.

"I staked out Riley's house last night. Lucas and Nora arrived in an Uber around eight thirty. I didn't recognize my husband at first. They were wearing raincoats. I followed them up to the house and peeked through the window. They were going at it in the center hallway. They didn't even bother to close the front door." A thought occurs to me. "She obviously wasn't worried about her husband coming home. I guess maybe Riley told her he was working late."

Ingram jots something down on a notepad. "How did you feel when you saw your husband having sex with another woman?"

I glare at him. "What're you, a shrink now? I was furious. What do you think?"

"Furious enough to kill him?"

"Hardly." I sip my coffee while I relive the moment. "I wasn't surprised, honestly. Our marriage was already on the rocks. I wanted to get the hell out of there, as far away from them as possible. I snapped my photographs and took off. It was pouring rain, and I wasn't paying attention. I stepped off the sidewalk into the wet grass, hence the muddy shoes. I got in my car and drove straight to my apartment and packed up my stuff."

When there's a knock at the door, Mel says, "That'll be for me." She grabs the backpack from the counter and takes it to the door.

Ingram and I stare daggers at each other while she's gone. There's something sinister about his golden eyes. He's handsome in a menacing way. I would not want to encounter him in a dark alley.

Ingram asks, "Did you come here after you left your apartment?"

I shake my head. "I went to Riley's office first. To confront him. I accused him of setting me up, and he didn't deny it." Mel returns and I shift my gaze to her. "Riley paid someone to kill Nora and Lucas. That someone just locked me in my trunk and ransacked my brother's condo."

"They're obviously looking for something," Ingram says. "Any idea what?"

"I don't know. I already gave him the photos."

"We'll get to the bottom of it," Mel says.

"Does this mean you're on the case now?" I ask.

Ingram jumps up. "No! She insisted on coming to find you when you didn't show up at the station. But she's not on the case."

I'm grateful for the distance separating us, otherwise I might strangle him. "Then you tell me, Mr. Detective, why isn't the media reporting on Lucas's murder?"

Ingram says. "Riley is an important man in this community. He's protecting his dead wife's reputation."

I slam down my coffee mug. "He's protecting his own reputation. He doesn't want his rich friends to know his wife was sleeping with a lowlife like Lucas." I look back at Mel. "Where is my husband's body?"

"At the coroner's office," Ingram answers for her.

Mel nods. "We'll have the report in a few days."

"Can we be done here?" I ask my old friend in a pleading tone.

"Yep." She gets to her feet. "Let's go, Calvin." She motions for him to follow her.

At the door, Mel says, "You can pick up your backpack from the station in a couple of hours."

Ingram hands me his business card. "If you think of anything else that might be useful, don't hesitate to call."

Locking the door behind them, I turn to face the apartment.

Jason will freak if he comes home to this mess. I get busy sweeping up the trash in the kitchen and straightening the furniture. I'm folding Jason's clothes into a drawer when he arrives home from the hospital ninety minutes later.

He tosses his backpack on the bed. "Are you doing my laundry now?"

"Ha ha. No. We had an uninvited guest. He left a bit of a mess." I fold his last pair of boxers and close the drawer.

"I assume this guest was here to see you. Did he take anything?"

"He destroyed my computer and camera, but as far as I can tell, nothing is missing. You should check your stuff, though. Just in case."

Jason moves to his closet and begins poking around inside. "And where were you when this happened?"

"Locked in the trunk of my car. Lucas is dead, Jason. He was murdered by the same person who killed Nora Riley."

Jason stops what he's doing and turns toward me. "I'm sorry, Jolie. I hated the guy. But I never wished him dead."

I lift a shoulder. "At least now I don't have to get a divorce."

Jason stares at me for a long minute. Sensing I don't want to talk about Lucas's death, he returns his attention to the closet. "I have homeowner's insurance. I'll replace your equipment and file the claim with the insurance company for reimbursement."

"You don't have to do that."

He removes his gun safe from the top shelf and punches in the combination. "Do you have money to buy a new computer?"

I stare at the floor. "No. But—"

"No buts. You need your equipment." He checks his gun and returns the safe to the top shelf.

"Thank you," I say in a meek voice.

Jason closes the closet door and comes to stand in front of

me. "Are you ready to trade in your profession for something safer?"

I manage a weak smile. "Where's the fun in that?"

He shakes his head, as if to say I'm beyond help. "Want me to drive you to the Apple Store?" he asks, his blue eyes twinkling.

I laugh out loud. "You just want an excuse to play with the toys."

"Can you blame me? I have so few pleasures in my life."

JASON and I spend longer than necessary at the Apple Store. Not because of me. I know exactly what I want—an updated version of my old laptop. But Jason, like a kid in a candy store, fiddles with every gadget on display. He's still wearing his hospital scrubs, and the attractive young sales associate fawns all over him. He eats up the attention and ends up purchasing an expensive iPad Pro.

In his Lexus on the way home, I ask, "Do you really need that iPad?"

"*Need* is a funny little word, Jolie. Besides, I have so few—"

"Pleasures in life," I finish. "Must be nice to have the money to buy whatever you want."

He glances over at me. "You could too if you went back to school."

"This may come as a surprise to you, but I have no interest in going to school for ten years to learn how to stick needles in people's arms."

"No one said you have to become a doctor. There are plenty of other respectable professions."

"Saving lives and sending criminals to jail is respectable."

"But you're not a police officer anymore. You're hiding in the bushes taking pics of rich men's cheating wives."

"Enough already, Jason. For the last time, I'm not going back to school." I turn up the volume on his WideSpread Panic playlist, and we ride the rest of the way back to town without speaking. I've been too preoccupied to consider how Lucas's death affects my finances. If word gets out I'm a suspect in a double homicide, my investigative career is over. With little money in the bank, I'll need to consider a career move soon.

When we exit off the downtown expressway, I say, "Can you drop me at the station? I need to pick up my backpack. I'll walk home."

"Don't be ridiculous. I'll wait for you." He drives several blocks and parks in front of the ugly gray building that houses police headquarters for the City of Richmond.

"I'll be right back." Jason stays in the car when I enter the station. I'm waiting for the rookie desk officer to track down my backpack when I encounter my old boss. I admire Captain Winnifred Byrd, known as Captain Winnie by her staff. She's an ex-marine who served several tours of duty in Afghanistan and Iraq. Never married, she's devoted her life to fighting crime. She's a no-nonsense straight shooter, and she has the respect and admiration of everyone in her department.

The captain comes from behind the counter to speak to me. "I hear your meeting with Detective Ingram went well."

I scoff. "Depending on who you ask."

Captain Winnie laughs. "He's tough but fair."

"That's exactly what Mel said. I haven't seen the fair side of him yet."

"I trust you to set him straight." The captain drops her smile. "Once you clear your name, which I have no doubt that you will, I'd love to have you back on the force."

"Thanks, but no thanks."

The captain places an arm around my shoulders. "Come on, Jolie. Don't you miss us a little?"

"I miss you a lot. But I don't miss having bricks thrown at me and people spitting in my face."

"The riots have stopped."

I let out a snort. "For now. They'll be back soon, now that the weather is getting warmer."

She drops her arm. "That's probably true. Will it help if I beg? I'm down fifteen officers. I'll make it worth your while."

"Let me think about it. I have more pressing issues at the moment."

The rookie returns with my backpack. "Everything should be in there."

I unzip the backpack and check the contents anyway. "Gotta run. I'll be in touch." I wave at Captain Winnie as I hurry out of the building.

"Thanks for letting me crash last night," I say to Jason on the way to his condo.

"Of course. What are brothers for?" He enters his parking deck and pulls into a vacant space.

I gather my belongings and get out of his Lexus. I'm heading to my car when he calls after me. "Wait! Where're you going?"

"To my apartment."

He follows me to my car. "Are you crazy? You shouldn't be alone right now. The lunatic who locked you in your trunk and ransacked my condo is still on the loose. Never mind you just lost your husband."

"I can take care of myself, Jason," I say, rummaging through my backpack for my keys.

He sweeps an arm at the elevator. "But don't you need to get your stuff?"

"I packed earlier. My suitcases are already in the trunk." Our eyes travel to the trunk. The metal is bent where Mel pried it open with a crowbar. "I'll need to get that fixed. For now, zip ties work for keeping it shut."

He sighs. "You're resourceful. I'll give you that." He opens the driver's door for me. "Please be careful. And call me if you need me."

"Will do." I get in the car and close the door. I watch him disappear in the rearview mirror as I exit the parking garage. I'd much rather stay here with my brother in his condo overlooking the James. But it's not fair to bring my danger to his doorstep.

Hunger pangs gnaw at my belly as I drive off down the street. I haven't eaten since dinner last night, and I need comfort food. The thought of a cheesy veggie pizza makes my mouth water. When I stop at a stoplight, I access the app for a food delivery service and place my order from my favorite pizzeria. But when I enter my apartment a few minutes later, nausea engulfs me, zapping my appetite. Memories of Lucas are everywhere. His running shoes beside the door. The gaming controller on the coffee table. The bottle of Texas Pete on the kitchen counter.

I drag my suitcases to our room. Bile rises in my throat at the sight of the bed I once shared with Lucas. The photo of Lucas and Nora remains on his pillow. He never saw it. Never came home last night.

I stumble to the bathroom and empty the meager contents of my stomach into the toilet. I flush and sit back on my haunches. I need to get the hell outta this apartment. But I can't afford to move. I'm not even sure I can afford to stay without Lucas's salary. Panic constricts my chest, making it difficult to breathe. How did my life become such a mess?

I return to the living room and pour two fingers of Casa Noble Tequila into a glass, sans ice. I'll need to cut corners. Which means a cheaper brand of tequila on the horizon for me.

The booze helps calm my nerves and settle my stomach. My pizza arrives, and I'm eating it straight out of the box while shopping online for digital cameras when there's a knock at my door. Removing my gun from its holster, I slide down the wall to the door and peek through the peephole. Calvin Ingram is standing outside, wiggling his fingers at me.

I crack the door. "What're you doing here?"

"The autopsy results came back from the coroner."

"That was fast."

"Riley pulled some strings. He's eager to bury his wife."

"I assume the report revealed something important. Otherwise, you wouldn't have come in person."

He nods. "Can I come in?"

I step back, opening the door wider.

He eyes the pizza box. "Sorry for interrupting your dinner."

"No worries. Want a slice? I can't eat anymore."

"No. But I won't turn down a shot of tequila."

I raise an eyebrow. "Liquid courage?"

"Something like that."

Sucking in a deep breath, I grab a glass from the cabinet and pour him a splash.

He gulps down the liquid and sets the glass on the counter. "Nora Riley was pregnant." Taking the bottle from me, he pours more tequila and kicks it back. "We ran a DNA test. Your husband was the father."

My knees go weak, and I brace myself against the counter. "Do you think Riley knew this when he hired me to follow them?"

"He claims he didn't. But we questioned Nora's best friend. According to her, Nora was desperate to have children, but Riley insisted he was too old. She's fifteen years younger than him."

I knit my eyebrows. "I was wondering about that. Was she his second wife?"

"Nope. He married late in life. She was his trophy wife." Ingram looks away from me, as though unable to look at me when he delivers the next blow. "According to Nora's friend, she was going to leave Laurence."

"For my husband." A stabbing pain lands in my gut and I drop to my abandoned barstool. I did this. I drove my husband away by refusing to have children.

"Jolie? Are you okay?"

"I'm fine." I push thoughts of my husband's bastard child away. I'm an expert at compartmentalizing my emotions, a skill I learned growing up in the foster care system. "So, Riley killed her to avoid handing over half his wealth in a divorce settlement."

"That's one theory. We don't know for certain he killed her . . . them. The coroner marks the time of death between eight thirty and nine."

My heart hammers in my chest. "I was at the Riley home at eight thirty."

Ingram strokes his chin. "Riley was still in his office when you went to see him. What time was that?"

I'd been too frantic, too upset, to pay attention to the clock. My mind races as I piece together a timetable. "I'm guessing around nine fifteen."

"Which means Laurence Riley could not have killed them."

I thumb my chest. "I didn't do it, if that's what you're thinking. Nora and Lucas were very much alive and screwing their brains out when I left."

"I believe you. I checked you out. Your reputation is stellar. You're off the hook. At least for now."

"Ha. My reputation for saving kittens from crawl spaces and little old ladies from muggers."

"Come on, Jolie. Don't sell yourself short. Everyone I talked to sang your praises. Why did you quit the force?" His gaze is penetrating as he waits for my answer.

I squirm and look away. "It's complicated."

"Being a cop isn't what it used to be." Ingram circles the apartment. "Your brother's condo suits you better."

"How so?" I slide off the barstool and stand on the other side of the coffee table from him. He's changed clothes since earlier. He's now wearing a polo shirt that clings to his tight abs and skinny jeans that hug his muscular behind.

"Beige carpet and walls versus exposed brick and stainless appliances. The condo has style. Like you."

"Wait. That sounds like a compliment. What happened to the arrogant Detective Calvin Ingram from earlier?"

"I'm willing to admit when I'm wrong about a person." Ingram unlocks the back door and steps onto the patio.

Following him outside, I get a whiff of his spicy cologne. He smells delicious, and I yearn to have a taste.

Jolie! Down, girl. You've had too much tequila.

Ingram studies the burnt chicken breasts on the grill. "Looks appetizing."

I close the grill lid. "Another dinner that ended in a fight. The story of my life with Lucas."

Ingram turns to me. "Your husband was a fool." His eyes are warm tonight, like liquid gold, and his touch is gentle when he fingers a lock of hair off my forehead. "You're beautiful."

Desire stirs inside of me. "So are you."

"I should go before I cross a line," Ingram says, but makes no move to leave.

"Are you sure? Won't you stay for one more drink?"

"I can stay. But a drink is not what I want."

THE SEDUCTION

My alter ego—the virtuous side of me that makes ethical choices—screams at me to resist Ingram's charms. He's the type of man who has caused me much heartache in the past. He will use me up and toss me aside. He wants my body, not my mind. I've been down this road more times than I care to remember. But I've been through so much these past twenty-four hours. My husband is dead. Is it so wrong of me to crave comforting?

When he hooks an arm around my waist and lifts me off the ground, I wrap my legs around him and let him carry me inside the apartment and down the hall to my bedroom.

Calvin is a skillful lover. But we're both hot and bothered, and it doesn't last long.

When it's over, I bite his shoulder. "That was intense."

He rolls off of me and stares up at the ceiling. "That was unprofessional. I rarely cross the line. Can we keep this between us?"

What a jerk. Then again, isn't this what I expected? "Of course. Thanks for the good time, Detective. I needed the release. I trust you can see yourself out."

He dresses and leaves the room without another word. When I hear the front door shut, I run to the bathroom and turn the shower on hot. I scrub every inch of my body, cleansing Detective Calvin Ingram from my skin. But he's still inside my head. Not Ingram himself, but what he represents. I've betrayed myself. In a moment of weakness, I succumbed to temptation. Last night, I pushed Drew, the good guy, away. And tonight, I jumped into bed with the devil. What is wrong with me? I'm deeply flawed. The hole in my soul is a festering wound that refuses to heal. If I let myself travel down that path again, I will fall off the cliff into the abyss.

I slide down the tile to my bottom and tuck my legs under my chin as water pounds my back. I was at a particularly low point in my life when I met Lucas. He saved me from myself. He accepted me for who I was, and I could be myself with him. But our courtship was short, our honeymoon even shorter. The insults began before the ink dried on our marriage certificate. Snide remarks he intended to be funny grew into full-on verbal abuse. When someone repeatedly calls you worthless, after a while you believe them.

I tolerated Lucas when I was still on the police force. When my life had purpose. When I helped people, saved lives, fought crime. When every day was different, and I was rarely home. In the beginning, Lucas and I were on the same page about not having children. It wasn't until I quit the force and started looking for a new direction in my life that Lucas decided he wanted children. I wouldn't consider it. I refuse to bring a child into this messed-up world. I drove him into the arms of another woman. Would I have changed my mind if I understood how badly he wanted a child? Probably not.

When the water runs cold, I wrap myself in my tattered terrycloth robe and make a cup of tea. I curl up in a chair in the dark living room to drink it. Lucas made a decent income installing HVAC systems, but he spent nearly every dime. We have enough in our savings account to cover two months' rent on this apartment. After that, if I can't find a way to earn more money, I'll have to move.

Placing my mug in the sink, I return to our bedroom. I need to know more about Lucas's relationship with Nora Riley. How long has he been playing me for a fool? Did he know she was pregnant? Was it an accident, or were they trying to have a baby together? I go to his closet and dig through his clothes. I find a lipstick, a garish pink that is definitely not my shade, in the pocket of his heavy coat. Which he hasn't worn since February and it's now early April, so they've been seeing each other for at least a couple of months. I find a pair of red lace panties in the pocket of his jeans. And, at the bottom of the hamper, in the pocket of a work shirt, I find a folded slip of paper, a printout of an ultrasound image. After an ink pen left in the pocket of his work pants ruined my favorite sweater, I'm always careful to check his pockets when doing laundry. Lucas knows this. He intentionally left this ultrasound image for me to find. This is his way of asking me for a divorce. Only someone killed him before I found it.

I'm tearing the printout in half when a pang of sorrow tugs at my heartstrings. While I don't want kids of my own, I'm an advocate for all children. I've witnessed horrific child abuse and neglect. This poor baby never got to take its first breath. Crossing the hall to my office, I rummage through the desk drawers for the Scotch tape. Taping the printout back together, I leave it on my nightstand as inspiration for finding this baby's killer.

Anger surges through me, and I go on a rampage, gathering all of Lucas's belongings into black trash bags and lining them up beside the door. I move on to cleaning the apartment. I vacuum and dust and mop. I wipe out the refrigerator, scour the bathtub, and change the linens on our bed. By the time I finish, the sky is brightening with the first rays of dawn. I walk through the apartment, admiring my handiwork. My closet is less crowded. Furniture surfaces are cleared of junk. The air smells fresh, like lemons. The negative vibe is gone.

I throw on some clothes, stuff my weapon and computer in my backpack, and load the black trash bags containing Lucas's belongings into the bed of his truck. Several years ago, he got a good deal on the gray Silverado by offering the previous owner cash. Now, based on estate law in the commonwealth of Virginia, the truck belongs to me. I can sell my heap to the junkyard for scrap metal.

I arrive at Goodwill before they open and deposit my contributions on the loading dock out back. On the way home, I stop at Starbucks for a grande black coffee. I'm gone forty-five minutes tops, and when I get to the apartment, I find my door ajar and the place ransacked.

Ugh. Not again. With weapon drawn, I search the house, but there is no sign of an intruder. And nothing appears to be missing. Fortunately, I took my most valuable possessions—my weapon and new computer—with me on my errand. *What are they looking for? Do they think I have evidence linking Riley to the murders?*

Dropping to the barstool, I turn on the local morning news while I finish my coffee, letting the caffeine kick in before I start the clean-up process all over again.

I freeze with the coffee cup at my lips when a familiar photograph appears on the television screen. I turn up the volume on the television. The same journalist who broke the story of Nora Riley's murder reports: *A new development in the Riley homicide case. Channel Ten News has learned an anonymous source has posted a series of damaging photographs to a dummy Twitter account. The images show an armed female, her face hidden by a black baseball cap, outside the Riley home around the time of the murder. Police refused to comment on the ongoing investigation.* The journalist goes on to provide background information about the murder of prominent attorney Laurence Riley's socialite wife. Once again, there is no mention of the wife's lover.

A blinding fury overcomes me. Whoever took those photos was spying on me while I was spying on Lucas and Nora. I'd be willing to bet this someone is the actual killer.

A pounding on my door startles me. "Police! Open up."

I click off the television and open the door. The same black female police officer from the day before, the one who retrieved my backpack from Jason's condo, is standing in my doorway. I note her badge. Jessica Bradley.

"I'm here to escort you to the station," Bradley says. "You're wanted for questioning in Nora Riley's murder."

I'm not surprised. Ingram can't ignore photographs like the one I just saw on TV. "I'll drive myself and meet you there."

The officer doesn't flinch. "Detective Ingram gave me strict instructions. I don't have to cuff you, but he insists you ride with me."

I study the woman. She's quite pretty, with flawless skin and piercing green eyes. "You're afraid of him. Why?"

"He has a reputation."

I wait for her to explain. When she doesn't, I say, "Let me get my bag."

Bradley calls after me. "Ingram says for you to bring your weapon too."

When I return, she holds out her hand, and I give the officer my holstered gun. We walk together to her patrol car. She opens the rear passenger door, but I climb into the front seat instead. She goes around the car and gets behind the steering wheel.

On the way to the station, I say, "Tell me more about Ingram's reputation."

"Everyone at the station is a little afraid of him. Ingram is . . . How should I say it? He's cunning. He says one thing and does another."

"So, he's a wild card. Which makes him dangerous."

Bradley lets out a sound that's half snort and half laugh. "Not in Ingram's case. He's only dangerous if you get on his bad side. I'd pick him for my team any day. He comes across as being unpredictable, but his moves are always calculated and controlled."

Calculated and controlled. I chew on this the rest of the way to the station. He came to my apartment last night with the sole purpose of seducing me. But why would Ingram want to control me?

At the station, Bradley shows me to an interrogation room where Ingram is waiting for me. He orders the officer to take my gun to the lab and motions me to the chair on the other side of the table. "Have a seat."

I glance at the chair and back at him. "What's this about, Detective?" I have no intention of making this easy for him.

"This." He opens a file on the table to reveal the photo of me yielding my gun at Riley's house two nights ago. "Care to explain?"

"I already told you everything." Planting my left hand on the table, I poke the photo with my right pointer finger. "I saw Lucas and Nora through this window. And I walked across the porch to this door."

"But you failed to mention the part where you drew your weapon."

I straighten. "For a millisecond, I considered shooting my husband. But when I saw him going at it with Nora, I decided he wasn't worth going to jail over. I took my pics and left the scene."

"I need to hear the story again." He gestures at the chair. "You might as well sit. We're likely to be awhile."

"Whatever." Seated opposite him, I start at the beginning, the part where Riley contacted me to take photographs of his wife and her lover, and I walk him through the events of that night. Not once. But three times. Ingram tries to poke holes in my story, and I answer dozens of questions. The interrogation lasts for hours. Ingram doesn't so much as offer me a drink of water. I have to pee, but I'm too proud to ask for a bathroom break.

It's close to noon when Bradley finally returns with my gun and the ballistics report. Ingram waits for her to leave before reading the report.

"No match?" I ask with a smug curve of my lip.

Ingram releases the paper, letting it fall to the table. "Inconclusive."

I spring to my feet. "I'm done here, Detective."

He stands to face me. "Not yet. Not until you explain this." From the same file, he produces the ultrasound printout of Nora Riley's baby.

My jaw hits the table. "Where'd you get that?"

It's Ingram's turn to appear smug. "It happened across my desk this morning."

"This morning?" I pace back and forth in the small room as I connect the dots. "I found that in the pocket of Lucas's work shirt when I was cleaning the apartment early this morning." I don't tell him I was up all night, ridding my apartment of Lucas. "When I left to take a load to Goodwill at around six thirty, the printout was on the bedside table. During the forty-five minutes I was gone, someone ransacked my apartment. Bradley dragged me down here around nine. Which means whoever broke into my apartment *happened* that across your desk."

His facial muscles tighten. "You didn't tell me someone broke into your apartment. Who was it?"

I stop pacing. "Duh. The same person who ransacked my brother's condo. The same person who killed Lucas and Nora."

"Why are you so hostile, Jolie? I'm not the bad guy here."

I glare at him. "I shouldn't have to tell you, Detective. Although I should tell the captain how you seduced your suspect."

He grunts. "Seduced you? Are you kidding me? You were begging for it. You admitted you needed the release."

"I was vulnerable. You'd just told me Nora Riley was pregnant with my husband's baby. And you took advantage of me."

He picks up my gun and stuffs it in his pants at the small of his back. Taking me by the arm, he says, "Come on. I'll drive you home. We can talk about this in the car."

I jerk my arm away. "No thanks. I'm done talking. I'll take an Uber," I say, grabbing the ultrasound printout from the table.

"What're you doing?"

"This belonged to my husband. Which makes it my property now."

He snatches the printout from me. "Sorry. But it's evidence in this case."

I shrug. "Whatever. You can keep it. I took a photo."

He gives me a hard look. "I'm driving you home. We have some things we need to get straight on." Taking me by the arm again, he ushers me out of the police station to his unmarked car.

Neither of us speaks until we're minutes away from the station. Finally, Ingram breaks the silence. "I got a text message from a burner phone minutes after I found the ultrasound printout on my desk." Whipping his unmarked car to the curb, he pulls out his phone and accesses his text messages. He holds up the phone so I can read the screen. *Tell the bitch to back off.* "You need to be careful, Jolie. You're in over your head. You don't know who you're dealing with."

"I know exactly who I'm dealing with. I consider that text a direct threat to me. Why did you just waste four hours of my time drilling me for a murder when you know that person"—I jab my finger at the phone— "murdered Nora and Lucas?"

He drops his phone in a cup holder. "Because I don't have evidence against them." He speeds away from the curb. "I'm under a lot of pressure to solve this murder, Jolie."

"Pressure from whom? The captain? Laurence Riley?"

Ingram shakes his head. "Higher up. Although I think Riley is ultimately making the decisions. He's proving to be more powerful than I originally thought."

"Riley is up to his neck in this. He hired someone to kill Lucas and Nora. And he's setting me up to take the fall." I turn my head away and look out the window. The stately homes pass in a blur as we race down Monument Avenue.

When Ingram arrives at my apartment, he takes his car out of gear and angles his body toward me. "If you get in over your head, I'm not sure I can protect you."

This sends a shiver down my spine. Officers protect one another at all costs. Unless he's a dirty cop. Which is not out of the realm of possibilities. "Who's pressuring you, Detective?"

Ingram lets out a sigh. "The mayor. Not the mayor's *office*. Stuart Moss himself."

"The mayor? Are you kidding me?" I bang my head against the seat. "I'm so screwed."

"I'm on your side, Jolie. I want to help you," he says, his tone touching on sincere.

"Like hell you do. You want to help me into a life sentence." I unbuckle my seat belt and open the car door. "If you really wanna help, you will stay outta my way. Sit back and watch, Detective. I *will* prove my innocence. In the process, I'm gonna take down Laurence Riley."

THE FUNERAL

Dressed in black, with fake designer sunglasses hiding my face and a brimmed hat covering my hair, I blend in well with the mourners awaiting the start of Nora Riley's gravesite service at Hollywood Cemetery. Being on the sacred grounds of the cemetery, where acres of rolling hills are covered with historic gravesites including those of two presidents, moves me. I often come here when I need a peaceful setting to calm my frazzled nerves. For whatever reason, whenever I'm here, I think of my mother. I don't even know if she's still alive. Today, I'm here for a different reason. To spy on the funeral goers.

As I move along the fringe of the crowd, eavesdropping on whispered conversations, I hear a woman with injected lips say to her friend, "Makes me sick to my stomach watching Laurence pretending to be distraught over the death of his beloved wife. Their marriage has been on the rocks for years. He knew Nora was having an affair."

The friend says, "Rumor has it she was planning to leave him. Laurence got off easy. Now he won't have to pay a divorce settlement. I heard the lover was her trainer."

Not trainer. The air-conditioning repairman.

I inch my way toward an older couple. The wife says, "Nora's mama is rolling over in her grave. She never approved of her marrying that man."

The husband elbows her in the ribs. "Shh!"

She lets out a squeal. "What'd you do that for?"

"Because Riley's a powerful man. We don't wanna be on his bad side."

I let out a grunt. A lot of people feel this way. Including the mayor.

The man gives me a dirty look, and I step away. Two men are talking in hushed voices behind me. "Why don't we just off the bitch and call it a day?"

"Boss says we can't. Not until we get the evidence."

Who are these men? Am I the bitch they're talking about? I'd have to turn my head in order to see them. That would be too obvious, and they might recognize me. The pastor announces the beginning of the service, and the crowd migrates as a whole toward the funeral tent. I use the opportunity to hide behind a nearby tree. From my new vantage point, I can watch the men. One is as tall as the other is small. Their cheap suits stand out among the well-dressed well-to-do.

The service is brief—a short eulogy with several readings. After the pastor says the benediction, I hold up my phone as though I'm reading a text and snap a half dozen images of Tall and Small. When they break away from the crowd, I follow at a discreet distance to where they park, making a note of the Virginia license plate number on their nondescript black Tahoe.

I walk the winding paths to the overlook at the mausoleum and stare out across the James River. I come here when I need to think a situation through. The water sounds from the rapids below help to clear my head.

The man's words come back to me. *Why don't we just off the bitch and call it a day?*

They had to have been talking about me. What evidence are they looking for? Something Lucas had? Or something I have? Then it comes to me. *The photos.* I palm my forehead. Why didn't I think of it before? I gave Riley a thumb drive, but I kept the originals on the memory card. Everything suddenly makes sense. The photos are more than evidence of Nora's infidelity. The photos are key to exposing Riley's involvement in his wife's death. In his wife's lover's death. In his wife's unborn baby's death.

Those pics are my lifeline. The public doesn't know about Nora's infidelity. About Lucas. But if they were to find out, and something were to happen to me, it would be awfully inconvenient for Riley if the wife of Nora's lover turned up murdered.

Energy surges through me. Game on! I know what I have to do. But I need a safe place to stay while I initiate my plan. And I know just where to go.

I get in the truck and speed back to my apartment. The new camera I ordered from B&H is waiting for me at the door. I toss the package into a duffel bag along with every piece of surveillance and podcast equipment I own. I pack some clothes in my suitcase and go into the bathroom for my toiletries. I dump my box of Playtex onto the floor. Among the tampons is my camera's memory card. I'm not surprised Riley's goons didn't find it. Men stay as far away as possible from anything having to do with a woman's menstrual cycle.

I lock up my apartment and throw my gear into the truck. Even though I detect no suspicious cars in the parking lot, I weave through the streets of the Fan, frequently checking my rearview mirror as I make my way to the West End. I stop at Libbie Market for provisions before heading out River Road to the Leonards' sprawling estate on the James River.

I've known Glenn and Gwen for a number of years. They pay me a small sum to check on their property while they're traveling. They are currently on an extended trip of Australia and New Zealand. While the grounds and buildings are outfitted with the most up-to-date security system, having me check on their home brings them peace of mind.

The main house doesn't appeal to me. The cavernous rooms filled with museum quality antiques and centuries-old portraits of ancestors give me the creeps. But I find the guest house out back charming. I stayed there once, for a long weekend when Glenn and Gwen were invited last minute to Nantucket and needed someone to keep their three corgis.

I let myself in the back door and pass through the kitchen and formal rooms to Glen's study. The paneled room offers sweeping views of the river and a wood-burning fireplace. I rummage through his desk drawers, locating an unopened package of five thumb drives. Slipping the package in my back pocket, I cross the room to his gun safe. Glenn is a gun enthusiast. We often shoot targets for practice at a range out in Goochland. He gave me the combination for his safe, just in case I ever needed it. I deem now as one of those times. Punching in the code, I open the heavy door and remove his semi-automatic rifle and a box of ammunition.

I retrace my steps through the house and out the back door. I drop my purchases and gear off at the guest house before parking the truck in the empty bay in the three-car garage. I unload my groceries in the small kitchen and set up my equipment at the square game table in the sitting room.

My first order of business is to copy the images onto three thumb drives, which I will hide around the Leonards' property later. I access the Channel 10 News website and recognize Kara Burgess as the young reporter on the Riley murder. The smug expression she wears in her profile pic takes away from her otherwise attractive face. I email her a simple message. *I have important new evidence in the Riley case.* I don't expect her to return my email on a Saturday afternoon, so I DM her the same message on social media. When she doesn't respond within ten minutes, I bombard her with information. I even tell her Nora Riley was pregnant with my husband's baby. Still no response.

I turn my attention to researching Tall and Small. I run the license plates and find the Tahoe registered to Ira Lopez. When I google his name, Tall's image pops up. I scroll through the pages until I find a photo of Ira with Small, identified in the caption as Manuel Rivera. I run background checks on them. Both come up squeaky clean. Too clean.

I thumb off a text to Mel. *I need a favor. Can you meet for a drink?*

She responds. *It's Saturday night and I have a hot date.*

Her second texts reads: *But I can meet for one drink.*

We go back and forth, discussing where to meet, until we decide on The Continental at six o'clock.

With still no word from Kara Burgess, I message her one last time. *This new development will make you a superstar.*

This time she responds. *Not interested. Stop harassing me.*

I blink hard as I read the message a second time. She's not *interested.* What reporter wouldn't jump at the chance to break a story like this? Something strange is going on here. And I aim to find out what it is.

I push back from the table and gather my belongings. I spend a few minutes hiding the thumb drives around the property before heading back to town in Gwen Leonard's white Mercedes sedan.

All the tables on the deck at The Continental are occupied, but Mel is saving a seat for me inside at the bar.

"Girlfriend, you look hot," she says. "What's the occasion?"

I glance down at my attire. I'm still wearing my black dress from the funeral. "I had a thing earlier today." I give her the once-over. She's wearing jeans and a loose-fitting white silk blouse unbuttoned to reveal a scandalous amount of cleavage. "You don't look so bad yourself. Who's the lucky guy? Someone serious?"

"Nah. He's a distraction. First aid to mend my broken heart."

"Are you kidding me? The ice queen finally fell in love?"

Mel lets out a grunt. "With the wrong man. I knew he was bad news. He's slept with every attractive female at the station. I just couldn't stay away."

My stomach sours. "Ingram?"

She looks away. "I don't wanna talk about it."

I decide it best not to tell her about my hookup with Ingram.

The bartender appears in front of them. "Ladies? What can I get you?"

Mel orders a wine, and I ask for a Casamigos on the rocks.

Mel waits for the bartender to leave before angling her body toward me. "You mentioned a favor?"

"Tell me what you know about Ira Lopez and Manuel Rivera."

She turns back around, facing the bar. "Never heard of them."

"We were partners once, Mel. I can tell when you're lying. I ran background checks. Lopez and Rivera are too clean. Something's not right with them."

Mel chews on her lip. I recognize this stall tactic. She's deciding how much to reveal. The bartender returns with our drinks, and we sip for a few minutes in silence. Finally, she says, "Lopez and Rivera are Riley's private security guys."

Mel knows more, but the firm set of her jaw lets me know she won't tell me.

A guy seated at the other end of the bar catches my attention. He's smoking hot with smoldering dark eyes and wavy black hair. Our eyes lock, and his lips part in a seductive smile. I hold his gaze for a minute before looking back at Mel. "Why is the media refusing to report on Lucas's death?"

Mel looks up from her wine. "You know why, Jolie. Riley owns the media, and he's protecting his wife's reputation. You need to let it go."

"If I let it go, I'm a dead woman. I overheard Lopez and Rivera talking at Nora's funeral today. There's a price on my head."

Mel's green eyes pop. "You went to Nora Riley's funeral. Are you trying to get yourself killed?"

"I'm searching for answers," I say, rattling the ice cubes in my glass.

Mel leans in close to me. "You don't know who you're dealing with," she says in an urgent tone. "These are dangerous people. Why don't you leave town until this thing blows over?"

"No way. Richmond is my home. Jason is here. And he's the only family I have. If I run, I'll spend the rest of my life looking over my shoulder. Riley dragged me into his mess. And I have to get myself out."

Mel lifts her wine glass. "Fine, then stay out of the way, and let us do our jobs."

"That's the problem. You're not doing your jobs. Riley had Nora and Lucas killed. Likely by Lopez or Rivera. Have you even brought them in for questioning?"

"We're following protocol," Mel says, which means *no*. She lowers her head, staring into her wine.

"What's happened to you? The Mel I once knew would never have turned a blind eye. Are you seriously going to let Riley get away with killing an unborn baby?"

Mel's head snaps up. "What're you talking about?"

"Nora was pregnant with Lucas's child. You didn't know?"

"I'm not officially on the case."

"Whatever." I slap my credit card on the bar and signal the bartender for the bill. When he arrives, I tell him to charge both drinks to my card. Mel objects, but I shut her up with a raised hand. "I got it."

The bartender returns with my credit card slip, and I sign it. I slide off the stool to my feet. "Thanks for nothing, Mel. If anything happens to me, you have my blood on your hands." I'm being melodramatic, but I don't care. I'm scared. And all alone.

Exiting the restaurant, I round the building to the parking lot. I hear footfalls behind me. I don't need to look back to know who's following me. When I reach the car, a husky voice says, "Hey, gorgeous."

I turn to face the smoking-hot guy from the other end of the bar. "What do you want?"

His fingers graze my arm. "The same thing you want. You gave me the look."

"What look is that?" I say, playing dumb. I totally gave him the look.

"The I-wanna-fuck-you look."

I roll my eyes. "You're delusional."

"Admit it. You want it. We can have a quickie right here." He pins me against Gwen's Mercedes. His breath is hot and reeks of whisky. I slip my hand in my purse and remove my pistol, poking it into his gut. "Take your hands off of me, or I'll blow your intestines all over this parking lot."

He jumps back, hands in the air. "Bitch! Put that gun down."

I outstretch my arms, training the gun at his chest. "Not until you leave."

"How do I know you won't shoot me in the back?"

"You don't. But you have a better chance of living if you run."

Spinning on his heels, he takes off across the parking lot. I laugh, loud enough for him to hear me. I'm proud of myself. The old me would totally have hooked up with him.

I get in Gwen's car and drive back to the estate. I change into sweats and return to my computer. I don't waste time trying to contact the other news stations. Mel said Riley owns the media. If they won't cover my story, I'll have to break it myself.

I start by going back through the photos I took of Lucas and Nora, choosing the ones I want to use and editing them to my liking. I'm removing the shadows in one photo when a figure pops out of the background. A large man standing in the hallway behind them with a gun in his hand. I zoom in on his face. The man is Ira Lopez. This is rock-solid proof of Ira's guilt. He's the murderer. The situation just got a hell of a lot juicier.

I download more images from the internet to make my video more compelling—snapshots of Laurence and Nora Riley at various social functions in addition to photos of their home and country club where they play golf and tennis. I set up my microphone and record the narrative of two lovers and their unborn child brutally murdered by the woman's successful lawyer husband. I work well into the night. The result is spectacular, if I say so myself.

I upload the video to every social media site where I have an account. Despite the late hour, it's Saturday night and people are still awake. I pour a glass of tequila and watch the numbers of likes and shares add up. My phone blows up with texts and calls from everyone I know. Mel and Ingram send urgent messages, insisting I call them back so they can protect me. *So now they want to protect me.*

Moving to the sofa, I catch a few hours' sleep with my hand resting on my pistol beside me and the semi-automatic rifle at my feet. I'm starving when I wake around eight. I scramble three eggs and brew a cup of coffee. When I open my laptop, I'm stunned to see my video has over a million hits. I read through the comments. Most wish me well and offer support.

My phone rings with an incoming call from my brother. Jason blurts out, "Where are you? I've been waiting for you at your apartment all night."

"Are you crazy? You're not safe there, Jason. Go home. Stay away from me until this is over." I push back from the table. "On second thought, Riley knows where you live. If he can't find me, he may send his goons after you." I take the phone over to the window and look out. Everything appears in order on the estate. "I'm at the Leonards'. Why don't I come pick you up? You can stay with me here for a few days."

"I can't miss work. And I can take care of myself. I'm due at the hospital, anyway."

"Good. Text me when you get there."

I've no sooner hung up with him when Mel calls. I don't answer the first time. But when the phone rings immediately again, I accept the call. "Jolie! Thank goodness. I've been so worried. Don't hang up until you hear me out. You were right last night. I have been turning a blind eye in this case. Riley is a seriously scary dude." She snickers. "But you let him have it. I think you're legit insane, but I'm proud of you."

"Thank you, Mel. That means a lot."

"Okay, listen carefully. You didn't hear this from me. Riley's on the run. We got a tip that he's booked on a private plane at ten thirty out of Richmond."

"Who gave you the tip?"

"Manuel Rivera, believe it or not. He turned on Riley. Not sure what that's about. We'll eventually find out. Anyway, we're on our way out to the airport now. I can't stop you from showing up with your camera. But be careful."

"I will. Thank you, Mel."

I grab my new camera, which is still in the box, and go to the garage for Lucas's truck. If bullets fly, I can't afford to pay for the damage to Gwen's Mercedes. While driving, I remove the camera from the box, insert the batteries, and attach my super-zoom lens. Reviewers on the B&H website rave about the video feature on this model camera. I'm excited about the opportunity to use it.

Midmorning traffic on a Sunday is light, and I make it to the private airport in record time. The scene is unfolding when I arrive. Through the window, I see Mel and Ingram having a conversation with Riley. Riley is gesturing with his hands, as though arguing with them. All eyes in the airport lounge are on them. No one sees Ira Lopez enter the building with gun raised.

Even though I'm no longer a police officer, I act instinctively. I draw my weapon and burst through the door, yelling, "Stop! Drop your weapon."

Rivera drops the gun, and his arms shoot up. Mel and Ingram are on him, securing the weapon and handcuffing both him and Riley. An army of patrol cars arrives at once, parking haphazardly around the building. I video the event, including the part where Riley snarls at me. "You're gonna pay for this, bitch."

I smile at him. "Looks like you're the one who's gonna be paying."

Mel and Ingram shove the twosome into the back of a patrol car, and they take off. The detectives make their way over to me. "We owe you one," Mel says. "A split second later, and we would've had a hostage situation on our hands."

"Or you would've been dead," I say under my breath.

Mel's radio crackles, and she holds it to her ear, listening. A second later she tells us, "Dispatch received a report of shots fired at Rivera's house a short while ago."

Ingram touches Mel's arm. "Let's go," he says, and they speed off in Ingram's unmarked sedan together.

Even though they don't invite me to tag along, I jump in the truck and follow them to a row house in the city's historic neighborhood of Church Hill. Units have already arrived. They crouch down behind their patrol cars when Mel and Ingram knock on the front door. When no one answers, Ingram kicks in the door. From my vantage point on the street, I can see a body on the floor in the living room.

Turning my back to the house, I raise my phone and click Video. The dead body is visible in the background as I record myself reporting on this new development.

Eager to feed my new followers, I race back to the Leonards' guest house and upload my video to social media.

I consider staying in the guest house a few more days. I could use some quiet time to myself, but I need to begin the process of putting my life back in order. I've established myself on social media, but my platform is a long way from providing income.

I pack up my belongings and secure the Leonards' estate. I'm on my way home when Chief Winnie calls. "I need to see you at the station."

"But—"

"Now," she says and hangs up.

The captain is waiting for me in her office when I arrive. I'm expecting a lecture. Instead, she offers me a job.

"I told you, Captain, I'm not interested in coming back to the department."

Her lips part in a mischievous smile. "What if I promote you to detective? You proved yourself by single-handedly bringing down Riley. I have faith in you, Jolie. You'll do a stellar job as a detective."

This gets my attention. My mind races. The position will give me financial security. I'll be able to move to another apartment and start a new life. And, to some extent, I could use my cases as material for my podcast. I'll invent a catchy name. *Fighting crime with Detective Jolene Hogan.* But what appeals to me the most is the opportunity to take down our corrupt mayor, who was so easily bribed by the likes of Riley.

"Can I take a few days to think about it?"

"Of course. In the meantime, call me if you have questions or want to talk more."

I stand to go. "Thank you for the vote of confidence, Captain. I promise to give your offer serious consideration. I'll be back in touch soon."

The morning chill has worn off, and the sun is warm on my face when I exit the building. I feel like skipping back to the truck. Riley and Lopez are behind bars. I'm sorry Lucas lost his life, but I'm grateful to have my freedom back. I drive over to the river and park on Tredegar Street. Grabbing my camera, I cross the footbridge and wander the winding paths on Belle Isle. I walk out onto the large flat rocks and snap a series of action shots of people rafting and kayaking down the river. On my way back to the parking lot, I pause at the top of the footbridge and shoot video of the rapids below to use on my website. I love this city I've called home for the past ten years. I'll do whatever it takes to protect her from crime and corruption.

I'm eager to get home, to begin work on my website, but there's something I have to do first.

While the afternoon is wearing on, Carrigan's is still hopping with the Sunday brunch crowd. My heart skips a beat when I see Drew through the window, hustling behind the bar. I long to go in and talk to him. I'm certain he's seen my video. Everyone in town has seen it. While we've never exchanged numbers, there are other ways to get in touch if he really wanted to. My hand is on the door handle when I change my mind. I'm not ready. I'm a broken woman. I slept with Ingram. Made a pass at Mr. Smoking Hot at The Continental. I can't drag Drew down to the swamp with me. I'm not worthy of being in a relationship with him. I'm in desperate need of healing. Although I have no idea how to go about the process.

FIREWORKS ON THE FOURTH

The first weeks in my new position as detective are uneventful. Chief Winnie gives me the department's cold case file to work through. Despite my best efforts, the results are underwhelming. The job isn't all bad. I enjoy working with Mel again, although I avoid Calvin Ingram at all costs. The salary more than covers my bills. I have my eye on a new apartment building in Scott's Addition with mostly young tenants, a hip vibe, and plenty of availability. I'm saving up to buy new furniture and waiting for my current lease to expire at the end of August.

Despite my large social media following, my podcasts are flat and few people listen. I wonder if it's the new job. Or if it's me. Maybe I'm not cut out for podcasting. Maybe I'm not cut out for law enforcement. If not journalism or police work, what am I meant to be doing with my life? I'm on a career journey. But I haven't reached my destination yet.

On Wednesday of the last week in June, Jason calls to invite me to dinner. "I've been seeing someone. And I want you to meet her."

I tighten my grip on the phone. I talk to my brother nearly

every day, and he never mentioned a girlfriend. "That's great, Jason." I wince at my halfhearted tone. Jason deserves happiness. I want him to find that special someone. But this means I'm no longer the center of his universe.

"Could you at least try to muster some enthusiasm? I thought you'd be happy for me."

I mentally scold myself for being selfish. "I am happy for you. In fact, I'm thrilled for you. When can I meet her?"

"Is tomorrow night too soon?"

"Tomorrow night is perfect. Where and when?"

We discuss the details for dinner before ending the call.

Jason and Stacy are sipping cocktails at an outside table when I arrive at The Daily a few minutes after seven the following evening. I'm expecting a nurse with a bubbly personality that matches her perky blonde ponytail. Instead, Jason's girlfriend is a striking beauty with boy-short dark hair, strong facial features, and doe eyes.

Introductions are made, and the server appears. I wait until he delivers my Casamigos on the rocks before I begin grilling her. "Where are you from?"

"Richmond. I grew up in the Near West End."

Which means she belongs to the country club set. "Where did you go to college?"

"Washington and Lee for undergrad. Georgetown for medical school."

She is from a moneyed family, for sure. The signs are there, not only in the expensive education but in her graceful manners —the way she carries herself and dabs at her lips with her napkin.

I sip my tequila with my pinky finger stuck out like I've seen wealthy people do in the movies. "What kind of medicine do you practice?"

Jason cuts his eyes at me. "Chill, Jolie. What's with the inter-rogation? She's my girlfriend. Not one of your murder suspects."

I fold my hands on the table. "As your sister, your only family, I feel obligated to check out her credentials."

Stacy pats his arm. "She's just looking out for you, Jason. I think it's sweet." She angles her body toward me. "I'm a pediatric emer-gency physician. My parents have been married for forty years. I have two younger sisters, both married with children. As far as I'm aware, neither Alzheimer's nor breast cancer runs in my family."

The server appears again. I allow my mind to wander while Jason is ordering the appetizers. I imagine Jason and Stacy as husband and wife, spending Thanksgivings and Christmases with Stacy's family at their mansion on Cary Street Road. Stacy's sisters, their husbands, and children. Cousins for Jason and Stacy's children to play with. The extended family Jason and I never had. Where do I fit in, the spinster aunt? Will they invite me to join them for these celebrations? I can hear Jason explaining to his in-laws about his pathetic sister who has no other family to spend the holidays with.

"When and how did you two meet?" I ask when the server leaves.

"About six weeks ago," Jason says, and Stacy adds, "My coworker, another ER doc, invited some people over for a cookout."

Jason places his hand over hers. "We hit it off right away. We have a lot in common."

I drain the rest of my tequila. "So, you've been seeing each other for six whole weeks, and I'm just now finding out about your relationship? That hurts, Jason. I thought we were closer than that." I sound like a bitch. But I don't care. My feelings *are* hurt.

Jason and Stacy exchange a look, but neither responds.

The server brings another round of drinks and appetizers to share—guacamole and fried calamari. I sit back in my chair and let Stacy do most of the talking. By the time our entrees arrive, I've warmed up to her. She's both hilariously funny and genuinely sincere. Hard as I try, I can't find anything wrong with her. As a detective, this would worry me. But as Jason's sister, I'm relieved.

My brother, the guy who used to scarf down his food, merely picks at his dinner. He's too preoccupied with Stacy to eat. He can't take his eyes off her. He's totally smitten, his adoration for her written all over his handsome face. Despite my earlier reservations, I'm thrilled for him.

When we finish eating, Jason and Stacy walk me to my car, and we say goodnight with promises of another dinner soon. I drive home to my apartment and spend another lonely night surfing Netflix.

I move through the next two days in a daze. I'm making myself miserable with this self-imposed mourning period. Why am I pretending to be sad when I'm angry as hell at Lucas for cheating on me? He got himself murdered by sleeping with the wrong man's wife. As for our marriage, I'd fallen out of love with him almost as quickly as I'd fallen in love with him.

I don't have to be alone. If Jason can find someone, so can I. Thoughts of Drew keep creeping into my mind, and on Saturday evening, I find myself outside of Carrigan's. The place is hopping, and Drew is hustling. I wait twenty minutes for a seat to open at the bar.

"Hey there, stranger. It's good to see you. I thought maybe you'd skipped town." His voice is soft, and his blue eyes twinkle. He missed me as much as I missed him.

"I've been going through some stuff. Lucas was murdered. You may have heard about it on the news."

He nods. "And I saw that badass video you made. You really

stuck it to Laurence Riley. I've thought about reaching out to you a million times. But I knew you were dealing with a lot. And I figured you needed your space."

"Yeah. These past few months have been rocky, but I'm feeling better now."

He tosses a paper napkin on the bar. "Can I get you a drink? Casamigos on the rocks?"

"I can't stay. But I wanted to see if maybe you'd have dinner with me sometime."

A lazy smile spreads across his lips. "Dinner would be great. In fact, what're you doing tomorrow for the Fourth?"

I shake my head. "I don't have any plans."

"My friend is having a party at his river house in Irvington. Pig pickin' and fireworks. You know the drill. I'm driving down for the day. I'd love for you to come with me."

"Did your friend include a plus one on your invitation?"

"It's not that kinda party. The more the merrier. Tim's parents' house is phenomenal. The party will be epic."

"In that case, count me in."

His face lights up. "Awesome. I'll pick you up at ten."

He slides his phone across the bar to me. "Text me your address and number."

I type the information into his phone and hand it back to him.

His thumbs fly across the screen, and seconds later, my phone pings with his text. *I can't wait to see you in your bikini.* He sends the message with a smiley face emoji.

Bikini? I haven't bought a bathing suit in years.

I tell Drew goodbye and exit the restaurant. Instead of going home, I make a run to Target for sunscreen and a bathing suit. I purchase a bright blue bikini with ruffle edges on the bottoms and a bottle of hot-pink nail polish.

At home, I give myself a pedicure and turn in early in anticipation of a full day tomorrow. I don't know when I've been so excited about a date. I'm dressed in my swimsuit and cover-up, with a canvas tote bag packed with towel and sunscreen, when Drew arrives at ten the next morning.

I answer the door, and he hands me a to-go cup from Starbucks. "Since you like your tequila neat, I figured you drink your coffee black."

I laugh out loud. "Bingo."

Drew drives a newish model Jeep Grand Cherokee. His GPS estimates ninety minutes of driving time. We have no shortage of topics to discuss. I tell him about Lucas's death and Riley framing me for the murder. Drew, in turn, talks about Carrigan's being short-staffed.

"Believe it or not, this is my first day off in over a month," he says.

"I believe it," I say with a nod. "We're down fifteen officers at the police department."

The party is already in full swing when we arrive. Tim's parents' sprawling house is on a hill with sweeping views of Carter's Creek. People and dogs are everywhere. Swimming in the pool, dancing on the deck, and playing Frisbee in the yard. We cross the grassy lawn and speak to Tim, who is overseeing the cooking of the pig.

Our host already has a buzz working, and he's hitting on a bleached blonde in the skimpiest bikini I've ever seen. Drew and I express our appreciation for inviting us to the party and move out of Tim's way.

"Do you want a beer?" Drew asks, gesturing at a plastic tub filled with ice and cans of beer.

"No, thanks. I'm not much of a day drinker. But you go ahead. I can drive home if necessary."

"I'm fine. I may have one later. I see my friend Jack down on the dock. Looks like he's headed out in his boat. Let's see if he has room for us."

Hurrying down to the dock, Drew waves at his friend as we approach the boat. "Hey, Jack! Good to see ya! Can you make room for two more?"

"Sorry, dude. We only have room for one. And I pick her." Jack nods at me with a mischievous smirk.

Drew cocks his head to the side. "Ha ha."

Jack motions us to the front of the boat. "Get in, man. It's great to see you."

Drew helps me on board. The three young women seated at the bow move over to make room for us.

Drew says, "Everybody, this is Jolie."

I wave as the other boat occupants introduce themselves.

"So, Jolie, are you from Richmond?" Jack asks, as he maneuvers the boat away from the dock.

"Not originally. But I've lived there for ten years."

"Jolie is a homicide detective with the Richmond City Police Department," Drew says with a hint of pride in his voice.

The pretty brunette next to me—I think her name is Terri—elbows me in the side. "Seriously? That is way cool. Can I see your gun?"

"I'm not carrying today," I say, even though my handgun is tucked away in my canvas tote.

As we cruise out of Carter's Creek, Terri peppers me with questions about the cases I'm working on. When we hit the Rappahannock River, Jack speeds up and Terri goes silent.

"Sorry. I probably shouldn't haven't mentioned your career," Drew whispers loudly near my ear, above the wind and motor.

I turn my head to his ear. "No worries. I enjoy talking about my job. As taxpayers, they have a right to ask."

Drew smiles. "Makes sense."

I settle back in the seat and enjoy the ride. I've only been on a boat one other time, and I find soaring across the waves with the wind whipping my hair exhilarating. We travel under the Rappahannock River Bridge and briefly enter the Chesapeake Bay as we make a wide turn around Mosquito Point. We go a short distance farther to a white sandy beach, which is already crowded with boats and people and dogs.

When Jack slows the boat, the wind dies, and I'm suddenly burning up. I slip my cover-up over my head, and I feel Drew's eyes on my body.

"Nice bikini," he says in a husky voice under his breath.

"You're so fit," Terri says. "You must work out a lot."

I smile. "I go to boot camp every morning at five." I let myself get flabby during the last couple of years, but when I rejoined the police department, Mel convinced me to go to boot camp with her. I'm stronger now than ever before.

Jack anchors the boat, and we all stand at once. One at a time, we crawl off the stern into the water, which is refreshing against my skin. Drew and I wade in the water and meander around on the beach. A cute girl with long golden curls offers us homemade spiked lemonade.

"What the heck? It's a holiday," I say, and accept the red Solo cup.

The beverage is tasty, not too sour or too sweet, but potent. I'm thirsty, and I guzzle it down. Combined with the heat of the sun, my head is soon buzzing.

For the first time in as long as I can remember, I allow myself to go with the flow and have a good time. But one is enough, and I pass when Goldilocks offers a refill.

Drew greets everyone by name and inquires about their families, significant others, and careers. He's the quintessential bartender, genuinely interested in people's lives. My fondness for him grows by the minute. When he takes his shirt off, revealing his muscular biceps and six-pack abs, a jolt of electricity travels through my body.

After we return to Tim's house, Drew and I find a hammock in the shade of a tree. I snuggle against his rock-solid body, and he tightens his arms around me. A gentle breeze tickles my skin as laughter drifts toward us from the party. Moments of pure contentment are few in my life, and I relish this one.

We doze off, and the loud clanging of a bell wakes us later.

"What's that?" I ask, scrambling to sit up. "Is something on fire?"

"That's the dinner bell," Drew says, pulling me back down beside him.

I place a hand on his bare chest. "Just so you know, I don't usually sleep with a guy on the first date."

Drew barks out a laugh. "Neither do I."

"Seriously, I'm sorry I'm not the life of the party."

"Are you kidding me? I'm having a great time. I, for one, really needed that nap. But it's getting late. And since we both have to work tomorrow, what say we get some food and head back to Richmond?"

"Sounds like a plan," I say, and throw my legs over the side of the hammock.

The line for the buffet is long. When we finally serve our plates, Drew leads me to a table with a lively crowd. Ninety minutes pass before we hit the road, heading home.

We're nearing Richmond when Drew says, "I'd like to see you again. But my work schedule is so hectic."

His words sting. He's blowing me off. And I thought we were getting along so well. "I understand."

He picks up on my disappointed tone. "No, you don't. I'm totally into you, Jolie. What I meant was, we might have to get creative. Would you be willing to meet me for breakfast one morning?"

A wave of relief rolls over me. "I'd love that. But I'll warn you, I'm ravenous after boot camp."

"I like a woman with an appetite. Will you wear your uniform?" he asks, his eyebrows dancing.

I play punch him in the arm. "I'm a detective, Drew. We wear plainclothes."

"Do you holster your gun on your hip or under your arm?"

I laugh out loud. "You've been watching too much television."

He turns on his blinker and pulls into my parking lot. "Until we meet again, we'll text each other, and I'll call you. We'll have late night pillow talk."

"I like the sound of that."

We get out of the car, and he walks me to the door.

"Thanks again for inviting me today. I don't remember ever enjoying the Fourth of July so much."

I press my lips lightly against his. When I draw away, he kisses me again. Our lips part and tongues meet. My body explodes like the fireworks bursting in the sky over the city from the baseball diamond.

He's adorable, and I want nothing more than to take him to my bed. But I don't want to scare him off. I give him another peck. "Goodnight, Drew," I say, and go inside.

After showering off the sweat, salt, and sunscreen, I put on my shortie pajamas. When I get in bed, I have a text message from Drew waiting for me. *Sleep tight.*

I respond. *Don't let the bedbugs bite.*

DURING THE FOLLOWING DAYS, I learn a lot about Drew from our continuous stream of texts. We have a lot in common. He never knew his dad, and his mom abandoned him at a young age. Out of the blue, she just up and left him in her sister's care. His aunt, a single mother of five, resented having another mouth to feed, and she took that resentment out on Drew. He kept to himself as much as possible, helped around the house whenever he could, worked hard in school, and got the hell out of there the minute he turned eighteen. Eric, his first cousin who works as a guest services agent at a five-star hotel in DC, is the only family he keeps in touch with.

Drew calls me late at night, his voice hoarse from talking over the noise of the crowded bar. He doesn't complain, but I sense his exhaustion. There's no end in sight for the long hours and overtime. His manager can't find employees for their many vacant positions—bartenders, servers, dishwashers. Offering a signing bonus fails to bring in candidates.

Drew and I finally find time to see each other on Sunday morning. We meet at nine o'clock at McLean's on Broad Street. When I order The Biggest Breakfast in Town without looking at the menu, Drew asks for the same.

As soon as our orders arrive, Drew gapes at the three fried eggs, sausage, grits, and biscuits filling the plate. "This is a lot of food," he says. "I'm not sure I can eat all this. Can you?"

I sink my fork into a fried egg. "Yep. I told you, I'm always starving after boot camp."

Drew pinches off a bite of biscuit and pops it into his mouth. "You went to boot camp on Sunday? Don't you take a day off?"

"Nope. In my line of work, I need to stay in shape." My gaze shifts to his muscular biceps, straining the cotton fabric of his shirtsleeves. "You obviously work out a lot. What do you do for exercise?"

"I run and lift weights. Lately, though, I'm lucky to get in a quick high intensity workout at my apartment."

"Are y'all still having trouble finding employees?"

He sighs. "It's gotten even worse. I threatened to quit if my manager didn't give me some time off. I have the whole day and night on Tuesday. Will you let me cook dinner for you?"

A smirk tugs at my lips. "That sounds like a health risk to me."

"Ha ha. You're funny." He tosses a sugar packet at me. "For your information, I'm an excellent cook. I've learned a lot from the chefs at Carrigan's."

I tilt my head to the side. "Oh really? Will you be serving fried mozzarella sticks for dinner?"

Drew laughs out loud. "I'll need to prepare a side of beef to satisfy your appetite."

It's my turn to laugh. "In all seriousness, you don't need to cook for me. We can go out. It's your day off. You should rest."

"I find cooking relaxing," Drew says. "Besides, I work in a noisy bar. I'm looking forward to a quiet evening at home."

I imagine a table set with candles and soft jazz music playing in the background. The thought of being alone with Drew stirs something deep inside of me. "That sounds nice. I'll bring some wine. Red or white?"

"Your choice. What time do you get off work on Tuesday?"

"Usually around five," I say, dragging my biscuit through a pool of egg yolk.

"Is six o'clock too early? If I sound eager, it's because I am."

I smile at him. "Six o'clock is perfect."

We clean our plates and linger over coffee. When he walks me to my car, he kisses me goodbye, a public display of affection that's out of place in the parking lot of a greasy spoon on a Sunday morning. But it's a promise of more to come. We'll have sex on Tuesday night. I'm absolutely certain of it. We both want it. We're both ready.

For the rest of the day, I perform my Sunday chores with my head in the clouds. I'm a bitch in heat, contemplating my hookup with Drew. Only this doesn't feel like a hookup. This feels like the real deal. Drew and I have waited a long time to be together. I have no doubt it will be worth the wait.

The tone of our texts changes in anticipation of our date. Our messages are suggestive, sometimes even naughty. On Sunday night, I go through everything in my closet looking for the right outfit. But my clothes are all blah. I need to go shopping. I can't remember the last time I bought something new other than the bathing suit I got for the Fourth of July.

I'm driving out to Short Pump Town Center on Monday after work when Jason calls.

"Can you meet me for coffee tomorrow morning? I wanna show you something," he says in a tone that is both mischievous and mysterious.

"Sure. When and where?"

"Eight o'clock at Stella's on Grove," he says without hesitation.

"Why Stella's? It's so out of the way," I say, changing lanes and exiting off the highway.

"Because I can't risk anyone seeing what I want to show you."

"Ooh. Now I *am* intrigued."

"Gotta go. See you tomorrow," Jason says and hangs up before I can interrogate him.

Laughing, I drop my phone in the cup holder. He's definitely up to something.

I meander through the stores until I find just what I'm looking for—a feminine and sexy yellow floral-print wrap sundress. On a whim, I splurge on a pair of Tory Burch natural-colored wedges. Thrilled with my purchases, I hurry home and try on my outfit in the privacy of my bedroom. I twirl in front of the full-length mirror, admiring how the dress dances about my thighs.

Drew's last text to me before I fall asleep is: *20 more hours until I see you.*

And another text awaits me when I wake for boot camp at four thirty the next morning. *14 more hours and counting.*

I channel my desire for Drew into my workout. I'm a beast, running faster and pumping harder until my lungs burn and my chest hammers against my rib cage.

When I arrive at Stella's promptly at eight, Jason is already waiting with coffee at an outside table. For once, he's not wearing scrubs, and I almost don't recognize him in khaki shorts and a striped polo shirt.

"What's up, bro?" I say, offering him a high five.

"You're in a good mood. What's the occasion?"

"I have a hot date tonight," I say, and laugh at his shocked expression.

He slides my coffee across the table to me. "Who's the lucky dude?"

"Just some guy I met." I'm not ready to tell my brother about Drew. "So, what's the big surprise?"

"Close your eyes and hold out your hand." I do as I'm told, and he places a solid object in my palm. "You can open your eyes now."

I stare at the ring box in my hand and back up at him. "What's this?"

He nods at the box. "Open it."

I crack the box and peak at the engagement ring inside—a large diamond set in a halo of smaller ones. I close the lid and hand him back the box. "I'm sorry, Jason. I'm your sister. I can't marry you."

"You're hilarious. The ring is for Stacy."

"I figured that." My smile fades as I think about my troubled marriage to Lucas. "Marriage is a big step, and the two of you haven't been dating long. Are you sure you're ready?"

He stuffs the ring box in his pocket. "Positive. She's the one. There's no point in waiting. I want her to be my wife."

"Then I'm happy for you," I say, my tone flat.

He reaches for my hand. "This won't change our relationship, Jolie. You're not losing a brother. You're gaining a sister-in-law."

He can say that all he wants, but nothing will ever be the same between us again. "Have you spoken with her father?"

"I took him to lunch yesterday," Jason says, sipping his coffee. "Her parents are great. I think you'll really like them."

"I'm sure I will. How're you planning to propose?"

"I'm still figuring that out. I wanna do something low key. Just the two of us. We both have next weekend off. I'm thinking of taking her to the Tides Inn or up to the Homestead in the mountains."

I knew it! He's already cutting me out of his life. I don't even get to take part in the engagement celebration. I mentally smack myself for being a bitch. Even though Jason didn't approve of Lucas, he supported me when I married him. I owe my brother the same respect.

He's grinning like the seven-year-old Jason I remember so well. I haven't seen him so happy since . . . Come to think of it, I've never seen him so happy. While we finish our coffee, we discuss creative ways for him to propose.

I give him a hug in parting. I don't want to let him go. He's my twin. My other half, the one person I've ever truly been able to count on. And now our lives are changing. He's getting married. I'm no longer the light of his life. But he's a good guy. He deserves a loving wife, a beautiful home, and amazing children.

A sense of dread overcomes me as I watch him walk off in the opposite direction toward his car, and for the rest of the day, I can't shake the feeling of impending doom. I tell myself I'm freaking out over nothing. Everything will be okay. Jason doesn't have cancer, and he's not moving to some faraway place like Europe. He's just getting married.

Excitement over my date with Drew returns when I'm in the

locker room after work. I'm retrieving my bag from my locker when an officer's radio crackles and dispatch announces, "Reports of an active shooter in the emergency room at Richmond City Hospital. All available units please respond."

The bottom drops out of my stomach. I click on Jason's number as I exit the locker room, and I'm relieved when he answers right away. "Thank God. Are you okay?"

"Security has us in lockdown in the surgical wing. But I'm terrified for Stacy. She's on duty. I need to get to her."

"No you don't! Stay right where you are and let us do our jobs. I'm headed to the hospital now. I'll call you when I get there."

"But—"

"No buts, Jason. Stay right where you are. I'm seriously not kidding."

HEROES AND HEROINES

With blue lights flashing, I speed through downtown to the Richmond City Hospital, screeching to a halt alongside the line of squad cars barricading the emergency room entrance. I spot Captain Winnie with a group of officers gathered beside a police van. I get out of the car and join them. "What's the latest update?"

"We're hearing reports of casualties," the captain says. "It's unclear whether they're patients or staff or both. The shooter is apparently strung out on drugs. We're waiting on a SWAT team."

I glance around the parking lot and back at my watch. "What's taking them so long?"

"I don't know," Winnie says in a tone of disgust.

I click on Jason's number. My call goes directly to voice mail. I try several times with the same results. I text him, but the text doesn't show delivered. "Damn it," I mutter under my breath.

Winnie's brow shoots up. "What's wrong?"

"Nothing. I'll be back in a minute." I head toward my car, and Winnie calls after me. "Where're you going, Jolie?"

"To check on something," I say over my shoulder.

Driving around to the parking deck on the back side of the hospital, I careen up four levels to the top where there are always available parking spaces. I know this hospital well. Not just because my brother works here. During my years as a patrol cop, I often had to follow up with suspects and victims who, after an incident, were brought in by ambulance for medical attention.

A member of the hospital's security team is stationed at the fourth-floor entrance. I flash him my badge as I barge past. The hospital executes periodic lockdown drills. The staff is well trained for catastrophic events, including natural disasters and acts of terrorism. This floor is reserved for post-surgical patients. The hall is quiet. There's not a doctor or nurse in sight. Are the patients aware of impending danger? Are they afraid?

Ducking into a stairwell, I take the stairs two at a time on the way down to the ground floor. The reception area, usually teeming with staff and visitors, is deserted. Unholstering my gun, I proceed with caution, passing through the empty food court where Jason and I often meet for lunch. I'm nearing the emergency room when I hear loud arguing. One voice belongs to my brother.

A shot rings out, and I burst through the double doors into the emergency room waiting area. A deranged man with stringy blond hair and tatted up arms is pointing a handgun at my brother, who is lying on the ground with blood seeping through his blue scrubs. My sudden appearance startles the shooter, and he trains his gun on me. I aim my weapon and fire. The bullet hits him in the middle of the forehead, and he crumples to the ground.

Stacy appears at my side from wherever she was hiding. "Thank God you're here. We need to get Jason into surgery, stat."

Medical personnel surround Jason, working on him as they

transfer him to a gurney. When they wheel him off, I follow alongside the gurney. "Are there any casualties?" I ask a nurse.

He gives me a grave nod and holds up two fingers.

Removing my phone from my pocket, I click on Captain Winnie's number. "All clear inside, Captain. The shooter is dead. There are two casualties. Jason has been shot. They're taking him into surgery now."

"What the heck, Jolie? How did you get inside?"

I end the call and power off my phone. I may lose my job for this, but I don't care. Jason is the only thing that matters right now.

I squeeze into the elevator with the gurney and staff. When we reach the third floor, Stacy directs me down the hall to the family waiting room. "I'll meet you there as soon as I know more."

Fear and anger rage through me as I pace the floor of the empty waiting room. I sit. I stand. I sit again, crossing and uncrossing my legs. I stand at the window, looking out at the tall buildings of downtown. I check my watch repeatedly. Minutes drag on. Five. Ten. Twenty. Around the thirty-minute mark, Stacy returns with fear etched in her face.

"He's in bad shape, Jolie. The bullet did a lot of damage. But he has the best possible team working on him. We need to pray."

Pulling me down beside her on a love seat, she lowers her head and begins reciting scripture. Jason and I have never been very religious, were never made to go to church as children, but I find the words comforting as I close my eyes and listen.

When she's finished, she raises her head and falls back against the love seat. "I don't understand. Why would he have risked his life like that?"

"To save you. I tried to warn him. I told him to let us do our jobs."

Her green eyes widen. "You talked to him? When?"

"I called him when I found out about the shooter. I told him to sit tight, that I was on my way."

"Where'd he get the gun?" Stacy asks.

"He bought it years ago. He has a concealed carry permit. He keeps it in his locker."

"I didn't know that. I don't approve of guns."

"Which is probably why he never told you," I say, wondering what else my brother is keeping from this woman he's planning to marry. "Jason is an excellent shot. I'm surprised he missed. Did he even fire off a round?"

Stacy shakes her head. "It happened so fast. He didn't have a chance."

"Because he's not trained. He should've waited." My brother's lack of experience may have cost him his life.

We fall into a deafening silence. Stacy and I are virtual strangers. Comforting each other would be awkward.

I'm acutely aware of the sounds in the hallway. There's a chorus of laughter coming from the nurses' station. How can anything be funny after what just transpired in the emergency room? Don't they know my brother is fighting for his life on an operating table?

I jump every time I hear the squish of approaching rubber soles on tile floor. A few of Stacy's colleagues stop in to check on her, but none provide updates about my brother's condition.

I stare at the wall clock. At six thirty on the dot, a sense of cold dread settles over me. Because of our troubled youth, Jason and I are closer than most twins. He's my other half. My intuitions about him are powerful. I instinctively know when all is not right in his world. And at this moment, I sense his presence leave this earth.

I brace myself for what's coming. For Stacy's sake, I need to keep my shit together. Moments later, the doctor arrives. His forlorn expression gives him away. When he delivers the news, Stacy lets out a blood-curdling scream and crumples to the floor. Taking her phone from her, I leave the room and go out into the hallway. I click on the top contact in her Favorites list, a female by the same last name whom I assume is her mother.

Marjorie Quinn answers the call, expecting to hear her daughter's voice. "Stacy! I've been worried out of my mind. Are you okay?"

"This isn't Stacy, Mrs. Quinn. I'm Jolene Hogan, Jason's sister. Stacy is fine. Jason is not. She needs you. She's at the hospital, in the family waiting room on the third floor."

I end the call and hand the phone to a nurse heading into the waiting room. "Give this to Stacy, please."

The walls close in on me as I flee the hospital. Exiting the parking lot, I burst into uncontrollable sobs. I can't face my empty apartment. And I'm too upset to be behind the wheel of a car. I drive over to Jason's condo and let myself in with my key. I go to his room and fling myself on his bed, burying my face in his pillow and breathing in the scent of his Old Spice body wash.

I howl into the pillow, pounding my fists against the mattress. A searing pain rips across my chest as my heart shatters into a million pieces. How did this happen? Only hours ago, he was seated across from me, with his little boy grin, informing me he was getting married. And now he's gone. I'll never see him again. Never hear his voice, that reassuring tone that made patients trust him.

I shed a torrent of tears until the pillow is sopping wet. How am I supposed to go on without Jason? I think of all the things he taught me over the years. To tie my shoes. To take up for myself, to fight back against those who tried to hurt me. To keep my chin up no matter how bad things got.

"Damn you, Jason!" I scream into the pillow. "You never taught me how to live without you."

Darkness has fallen over the room by the time I raise my head. Throwing my feet over the side of the bed, I make a dash for the bathroom and puke up my guts. I curl up on the cool tile floor and sob my heart out. I need something for the pain, the ache of a five-ton elephant stomping on my chest. Grabbing hold of the sink counter, I pull myself up and open the medicine cabinet. Advil is the strongest Jason has. I swallow three tablets without water. I consider consuming the entire bottle. But Advil won't do the job.

I stumble back to Jason's bed. I shouldn't be alone right now. I power on my phone. I have many missed calls and texts from Captain Winnie and Mel. Even Detective Ingram messaged me. And Drew. I forgot all about our date. I thumb through his string of texts. He knows about Jason from the news. I should go to him, let him comfort me. But Drew is not who I need right now. I need Jason right now. I need my brother to walk in the door and tell me his death was all a big mistake.

I turn the phone off and plod on bare feet down the hall to the living area. Removing a bottle of tequila from Jason's liquor cabinet, I pour two fingers into a glass. I sniff it and set it down on the counter. Tequila is not what I need either.

Someone pounds on the door. When I open it, I'm shocked to see Ingram standing in the hallway.

"I've been looking for you, Jolie. I went to your apartment. When you weren't there, I figured you might be here."

He extends his arms, and bursting into tears, I fall into them. Closing the door behind us, he walks me backward to the sofa. I cry with my face pressed against his chest until his shirt is soaked through.

The intense emotions pulsing through me reach a manic level. I tug Ingram's shirt over his head and unbutton his jeans. I strip off my clothes, push him down on the sofa, and straddle him. He enters me, and for a few brief moments, as I ride him hard, I feel something other than pain. I climax and collapse on top of him. After a minute, I roll off of him onto my back. "I'm so sorry, Ingram. I'm not myself right now."

"No need to apologize. But you took me by surprise. I didn't use protection."

"I'm on the pill." I think about all the women in the department he's been with. "Are you clean?"

"As far as I know. I'm usually diligent about using a condom."

I expect Ingram to leave like last time. Instead, he yanks the throw blanket off the back of the sofa and drapes it over us. He holds me close, stroking my hair. "I understand what you're going through, Jolie. My sister died in a car accident when we were in college. A drunk driver killed her. We weren't twins. But we were Irish twins, fourteen months apart."

I push myself up so I can see him. "That's awful. I'm so sorry. What was her name?"

"Alyssa. I wish I could say I'm over it, but I'm not. It's been ten years, and I still miss her every single day." His golden eyes shine with unshed tears.

"No one ever told me."

"No one knows. I don't talk about her. It's too painful. But I remember the day she died like it happened yesterday. I thought you might need a friend. Have you called your family?"

I shake my head. "Jason was my only family." My throat hitches, and more tears spill from my eyes. "We never knew our father. And our mother took off when we were kids. We were raised in the foster care system. Somehow, we stayed together."

"You can't do this alone, Jolie. For the next few days, I'm your family. But you have to stop calling me Ingram. I have a first name."

I press my lips into a smile. "Calvin. I have no clue what I'm supposed to do. How does one go about planning a funeral?"

"I'll help you." Calvin sits up and gathers his clothes. "Jason was much loved by his friends and coworkers at the hospital. The media is calling him a hero. There's already a memorial of flowers and balloons and cards at the emergency room entrance."

This brings on a torrent of tears. "When will this crying stop?"

Calvin hands me a box of tissues. "Not anytime soon." He gets dressed and goes over to the kitchen. "You need to eat." He opens the refrigerator door. "How about an omelet?"

I scramble to put on my pants. "I can't think about eating right now." Not when Jason will never take another bite of his favorite foods.

He closes the refrigerator door. "You'll get sick if you don't eat. These next few days and weeks will be about surviving." He eyes the tequila bottle. "You can't wallow in self-pity, Jolie. Don't let the grief get a hold of you. I tried to drown my sorrows, and it nearly killed me. My parents' marriage didn't survive. My mother is doing better now. She's a strong woman. But my father is drinking himself to an early grave."

I move to the island, watching as Calvin steeps two cups of chamomile tea. He doesn't strike me as the tea type. He's full of surprises tonight.

Seated together at the island, we make a long and detailed list of things I need to tend to in the coming days.

Planting my elbows on the bar, I bury my face in my hands. "There's so much to do. It's overwhelming."

"Going through the process of burying your brother will distract you from your grief. You'll get to spend time with his friends, which you'll find comforting." Calvin slides off his barstool and pulls me to my feet. "You need some sleep. Let's get you in bed."

I doubt I'll be able to sleep, but I let him lead me down the hall to the bedroom, anyway. He rummages through Jason's drawers for a T-shirt and tosses it to me. "Here. Change into this."

I go into the bathroom and close the door. I strip off my clothes and pull the T-shirt over my head. It smells like Jason's fresh-linen laundry detergent, and I stand there with my nose pressed against the fabric, looking at my haunted reflection in the mirror. I finger-brush my teeth, and pee, and when I exit the bathroom, Calvin has pulled back the covers and is standing beside the bed.

I climb in and he tucks the covers around me. "I'll be in the living room if you need me."

I look up at him. "You're staying?"

"I'm certainly not leaving you alone. Not tonight." Turning out the bedside table lamp, he leaves the door cracked on his way out of the room.

I toss and turn for over an hour before finally dozing off. A nightmare startles me out of a deep sleep sometime later. I sit bolt upright as the dream comes back. I'm in the emergency room. I'm aiming my gun at the shooter, only the shooter is Jason. I pull the trigger, and my brother drops to the floor.

Throwing back the covers, I hurry down the hall to the living room. Calvin is sitting on the sofa, staring out the window into the dark night while holding a glass of golden liquid, which I assume is bourbon.

He doesn't hear me, and when I say his name, he startles. "Jolie. I thought you were asleep."

I sit down close to him. "I had the worst nightmare."

He drapes an arm around my shoulders. "Wanna talk about it?"

I shake my head. "I never want to think about it again."

"Better get used to it. There will be many more to come." A faraway expression settles over Calvin's face. "But you'll have pleasant dreams too. Ones that bring Jason back to you, leaving you all warm and fuzzy inside."

I cut him a sideways glance. "Warm and fuzzy? Who are you, and where did Detective Calvin Ingram go?"

He chuckles. "I'm not the hard-ass you think I am. I have a soft side." He drops his smile. "I just don't let people get too close."

"Because of Alyssa?"

"Yep." He reclaims his arm. "You're a better person than me. A more loving person than me. Don't close off your heart like I did."

I tilt my head to the side. "Do as I say, not as I do?"

He grunts. "Something like that."

We talk for a while about where people go when they die and how hard it is for those left behind to move on with their lives. We fall asleep with our heads resting against the back of the sofa. When I wake in the morning, Calvin is gone. But I find a note from him beside the coffeemaker. *Gone home to shower and change. You should do the same. Get started on your list. I'll check in with you soon.*

I eye the tequila bottle on the counter. I can start planning my brother's funeral, or I can drink myself into a stupor. I pick stupor. I can't stand this agony. But as I'm uncorking the cap, my brother's image flashes before me. His golden hair and sparkling blue eyes. His charming smile that won over everyone he ever met. Calvin's words come back to me. *Jason was much loved by his friends and coworkers at the hospital. The media are calling him a hero. There's already a memorial of flowers and balloons and cards at the emergency room entrance.* I'll give him a proper burial first. Then, I'll fall apart.

While I drink my coffee, I contact the funeral home and make arrangements to have Jason's body cremated, which is the one thing I'm certain Jason would want. The funeral director assured me he could help prepare for the memorial service. When I hang up, I give myself a pat on the back for making it through the first call without breaking down.

Draining the rest of my coffee, I change into yesterday's clothes and drag myself out the door. Jason's presence is strong in his condo. Leaving here is like losing him all over again.

Back at my apartment, I take a long hot shower and flip through the clothes in my closet. In defiance of the traditional black mourning attire, I choose white jeans and a pale blue sleeveless top. My clothes are not about my loss. Jason knows my heart is heavy. My outfit is a message to him. I want him to know he was the light in my life.

Filling two suitcases with clothes, toiletries, and electronics, I toss them into the trunk of my unmarked car and drive to the hospital. Jason's memorial occupies the length of sidewalk in front of the emergency room. I pause for a few minutes to read the cards and messages his friends, patients, and coworkers have left. More tears are just beneath the surface, but somehow, I keep them at bay.

I find Frankie Collins, the hospital chaplain and a friend of Jason's, in his office. We pray together, and then talk for a minute about what a great guy my brother was. He agrees to preside over the memorial service and suggests I hold off until Saturday when more hospital staff and administration can attend.

With the help of a security guard, I clear out Jason's locker before leaving the hospital. I'm on the way to Hollywood Cemetery when Calvin calls. "How're you holding up?"

"Hanging in there. I'm tackling my list," I say as I exit the downtown expressway onto Belvidere Street. "You were right. The distraction helps."

"Where are you now?"

"I just left the hospital headed for Hollywood Cemetery."

"I'll meet you there," Calvin says and ends the call before I can argue.

At the cemetery, I only have to wait a few minutes before Calvin arrives. My meeting with the cemetery staff member doesn't take long. I know exactly what I want—a granite niche to house Jason's cremated remains. She provides the options for location, and I pick one offering a sweeping view of the James River. Jason won't see it. But I will when I visit him. And I plan to spend a lot of time here.

My eyes go wide when she tells me the price, which is more money than I have in my savings account. But I'll worry about how to pay for the burial expenses later. I'll go into debt if need be. I want the best for my brother.

Calvin walks me to my car afterward. "The captain wants to see you sometime today. She understands you need time off, but she has to file your official statement about yesterday's events."

Yesterday's events. I'm not ready to rehash the shooting. But I won't be able to put Captain Winnie off. I'm surprised she's given me this long. I click the doors unlocked. "I need to return this unmarked car, anyway. Tell her I'll stop by in a while. I have to take care of something first."

"Do you want me to come with you?" His features are soft, his expression concerned. Calvin Ingram is not the man I thought he was.

"No. But thanks. This is something I have to do alone." I slide behind the wheel and speed off, leaving Calvin standing in the parking lot.

As I expected, Stacy's parents live in a stately home on Cary Street Road. A uniformed housekeeper greets me at the door and motions me to the backyard where Stacy is lounging in the shade of a pink crape myrtle tree. Despite the heat, she's wearing a pink terrycloth robe and dark sunglasses that covers much of her face. She appears to be asleep with her mouth ajar, but when I approach, she straightens her chair to an upright position.

"This sucks," she says. "I can't eat. Can't sleep. I keep having panic attacks, even though I've taken enough Xanax to bar out a giant. And I'm only the girlfriend. I can't imagine what you're going through."

"You were more than his girlfriend, Stacy. Jason would want you to have this." I place the ring box in her lap.

She looks at the box and back up at me.

I ease down to the lounge chair beside her. "Jason and I met for coffee yesterday morning. He was a kid in a candy store when he showed me that. He'd already spoken with your father, and he was planning to propose this weekend."

Stacy opens the box and gasps. A tear slides down her cheek from under her sunglasses. "I can't accept this, Jolie. Take it back to the jeweler. Use the money for his funeral."

"I'm not worried about the funeral expenses," I lie. "Jason bought the ring for you. You should keep it to remember him by."

"As if I could ever forget him." She removes a wadded tissue from her pocket and wipes the tears that are now streaming down her face. "Jason adored you. I'm sorry we never got to be sisters."

We talk for a few minutes about what might have been, and by the time I stand to leave, we are both bawling like babies. She walks me to the door. "At some point, I need to get my things from his condo."

"Just let me know when. I'll make a point of not being there, so you can have some time alone."

Stacy's words rush back to me as I head back downtown. *I'm sorry we never got to be sisters.* I'm sorry about so many things that will never happen. I'll never get to see Jason and Stacy walk down the aisle. I'll never get to meet my niece or nephew, the children Jason so desperately wanted. Since I won't be having children of my own, I'm the end of the line for my family now. There is no one else. Only me. Jason left me to face the world alone.

SPIRALING

The days preceding Jason's funeral pass in a blur. His friends plan a get-together for Friday night to comfort one another. While I've met many of them, I don't consider any my friends. They include me out of respect for Jason, and I attend for the same reason. I expect a cryfest, but instead of bringing me down, their love for my brother warms my heart, and the anecdotes they tell about him boost my spirits.

The morning of Jason's funeral dawns with oppressive humidity. At eleven o'clock, a larger than expected number of mourners gather around the tented area for the brief service. The cemetery is set on a hill above the James River where Richmonders sunbathe on rocks and kayak down the rapids like any normal summer Saturday. For me, today is the worst day of my life, a Saturday I won't soon forget.

I'm wearing the yellow sundress I bought for my date with Drew. I don't care if I stick out like a sore thumb in a sea of black. I want to look pretty for my brother. And I'm not the only one. I smile to myself when Stacy shows up in a short-sleeve emerald-green sheath.

When we hug, she says, "I feel his presence. He's smiling down on us, willing us to be strong."

During the service, I spot Drew at the back edge of the crowd, looking handsome in a charcoal-gray suit. He's left countless messages on my cell phone, his tone urgent as he pleads for me to call him back. How can I think about romance when my brother is dead?

Drew approaches me after the service, and we share an awkward embrace. "I don't know what to say, Jolie. Sorry seems inadequate. I know how much your brother meant to you. I'm here for you if you need me."

"Thank you. I apologize for not responding to your messages. I've been focused on getting through the funeral. I have no idea what comes next for me. I need some time."

Drew's shoulders slump. This is not what he wants to hear. "I understand."

Calvin appears from nowhere. Taking me by the elbow, he leads me away from Drew and over to his car. I feel Drew's eyes boring a hole in my back. The last thing I want to do is hurt him. But he's better off without me. I'm a mess. I can't see myself being ready for a relationship anytime soon.

True to his word, Calvin has been my rock these past few days. He checks in with me frequently and sleeps on Jason's sofa at night so I won't be alone. We have long talks about the grieving process and how one moves on after a profound loss. The animosity I've felt toward him over these past few months is waning, and an easy friendship is developing between us. We now have something in common. We've formed our own private club—The Dead Siblings Society. Calvin doesn't open up to many people, and his vulnerability is a gift I cherish.

Stacy's parents host a catered reception with an open bar and elaborate spread of food. Marjorie and Edgar Quinn are an elegant couple in their late fifties. When I express my gratitude for their hospitality, Marjorie says, "It's the least we can do. We adored Jason. He was a generous soul. He will be missed."

Edgar gives his head a solemn nod. "I was thrilled about the prospect of having him as a son-in-law. I was determined to make him a golfer."

"He would've been an eager student. Golf is the one game Jason always wanted to master but never had the time." The image of Jason playing golf with Arnold Palmer in heaven brings a smile to my face.

A young man who introduces himself as Jason's attorney drags me to the corner of the pool. Jason mentioned Chris Bates once, when I asked my brother if he knew a good divorce attorney.

"Jason had me draw up his will a few years ago," Chris says.

I give him an incredulous stare. "His will? But he was so young."

"He was doing me a favor," Chris says. "I'd just passed the bar exam, and he wanted to throw me some business."

I smile. "That sounds like Jason."

"The document is straightforward. You're the only recipient of his estate."

I shake my head, unsure I heard him correctly. "What estate?"

"The equity in his condo, and a decent size savings account. He made good money these past few years."

"Right. And he worked too hard to spend it."

"The estate will go to probate court, but I can arrange for an advance if you need money to cover the funeral costs and make mortgage payments. Call me when things settle down." Chris hands me his business card and wanders off.

I'm still standing beside the pool, staring down at his card, when Captain Winnie joins me. "I've gotta run, baby. But I couldn't leave without speaking to you first. I want you to take all the time off you need. However, in my experience, work is the best medicine in cases like these."

The best medicine, I think. If only I could pop a pill from a bottle labeled *work,* and all my pain would go away.

I smile because I don't know what to say. I can't fathom going back to work anytime soon. When Lucas died three months ago, my grief was nothing like this. I felt sad about the loss of his life. But he was cheating on me, and our marriage had been over for some time. The pain of losing Jason is unbearable. I can't focus, can't think straight. How could I possibly interrogate suspects and solve crimes?

On the way home, Calvin gives me a lecture about moving on with my life. I tune him out. I have only one thing on my agenda for the foreseeable future. Drinking. Heavily. When we reach the parking garage, he turns off the car and moves to get out. I grab his arm. "I need some time alone, Calvin. Thanks for all you've done for me these past few days. I wouldn't have survived without you. But you don't have to babysit me anymore."

He thumbs my cheek. "I don't think of it as babysitting. I think of it as helping a friend in need. I'll respect your privacy. But I *will* be checking on you."

"I'm counting on it," I say, kissing his cheek.

I get out of the car and walk over to the elevator. Instead of going up to the condo, I ride the elevator down to the underground level, where I parked my truck.

I drive to the liquor store, load up on tequila, and go on a five-day bender. I drink. I sleep. I cry. When my phone battery dies, I don't charge it. I don't open my laptop. Don't check my emails. I go days without showering. My body is numb, my brain in an alcohol haze.

Around eight o'clock on Thursday night, Calvin pounds on my door.

"Jolie, I know you're in there. I'm worried about you. Why aren't you answering my calls and texts? I need to know you're all right."

I stare at the door without opening it.

"Fine. I'll give you another twenty-four hours. If I don't hear from you, I'm coming back and kicking the door down."

I drain the remaining tequila in my glass. Sliding off my barstool, I dart across the room and throw open the door in time to see Calvin disappear into the elevator. I could go after him. He would give me what I need. But it's just as well. I now consider him a friend. And I make a point of not sleeping with friends.

I return to the kitchen and pour more tequila in my glass. Jason is the only one who knows about my sordid past. And he took that knowledge with him to the grave.

There was a period in my life, in my late teens and early twenties, when I slept with any man who crossed my path. Jason, recognizing the pattern as self-destructive, insisted I see a therapist. After six months of weekly sessions, she determined my reckless behavior stemmed from my mother abandoning me at such a young age. Another six months of cognitive behavioral therapy and I had given up promiscuous sex. Three months later, I met Lucas.

My craving is intense. I'm a crack addict in need of a fix. In three months, I've lost my husband and my brother. I'm expected to fall into bad habits.

For the first time since Jason's funeral, I leave the condo. I take an Uber to a popular Irish pub in Shockoe Slip. A rowdy crowd has pushed together several tables, but there are plenty of seats open at the bar. I've been drinking since noon, and I slur my words when I order a tequila neat from the pretty young bartender.

She gives me a skeptical look. "Sounds to me like you've had enough already."

"I'll nurse it. Promise," I say, fingering a cross over my heart.

She brings me the drink, and I take a baby sip. Glass in hand, I spin around on the barstool. My vision is blurry, and I close one eye to focus. All the occupants of the rowdy table are guys. Seriously hot guys. I lock eyes with a tall blond who's standing at one end of the table as though preparing to leave.

He moseys over and gestures at the empty stool beside me. "Is this seat taken?"

I smile up at him. "By you."

He sits down beside me, and I spin around to face the bar. "Can I buy you a drink?" he asks.

I lift my half-empty glass. "I'm fine. But thanks." I yearn to drain the tequila, to ask for another. But I won't embarrass myself by having the bartender refuse to serve me.

He touches his nearly empty beer mug to my glass. "I'm Russell," he says, but he doesn't ask my name. He's just what I'm looking for. A no-strings-attached roll in the hay.

We make small talk while he finishes his beer. Despite his blond good looks, I sense a wickedness lurking within. Good! I like them naughty.

Desire pulses through me when he says, "What say we get outta here, go somewhere quieter?"

I toss my thumb over my shoulder. "What about your friends?"

He dismisses them with a flick of the wrist. "Those are just some guys from work. I was getting ready to leave anyway."

"Awesome." I pay my tab, and we exit the pub together.

I stumble on the way out, and he grabs my arm, preventing me from falling. "I hope you're not driving."

"Nah. I Ubered here."

"Cool. My car's around back." I follow him around the side of the building and down a short alley to a silver sedan in the small parking lot. He shows me to the passenger side. I'm thinking he's a gentleman, helping me into the front seat, when he opens the rear door and pushes me inside. He dives in on top of me, leaving the door open with his feet sticking out.

He's biting my neck and pawing at my body. He tears my blouse open, the buttons flying in all directions, and tugs at my bra. I sober up fast. He's going to rape me if I don't stop him. I try to fight back, and he slaps me hard across the face.

"You know you want it, you whore."

I manage to twist an arm behind me. When my hand connects with the butt of my pistol, I say a silent prayer of gratitude.

Freeing the weapon from my waistband, I dig the tip of the barrel into his belly. "Get off of me or I'll blow your guts all over the roof of your car." Watching his blue eyes grow wide in fear gives me great pleasure.

Russell throws his hands in the air. "I swear, I wasn't going to hurt you."

"Like hell you weren't. You were going to rape me." I jab the gun at him as he scrambles out of the car. He's on his feet, zipping up his pants, when I slide across the seat and kick him in the nuts with the heel of my cowboy boot. He screams and doubles over in pain. I get out of the car and karate chop him in the side of the neck. He falls to the ground, and I kick him in the ribs with my pointy toe. "Take that, you miserable prick."

Holding my torn blouse together, I take off running back down the alley to Cary Street. I spot a Richmond City squad car idling at the corner. I approach the car on the passenger side and tap on the window. I'm relieved to see the officer is my old friend, Leo McCormick. He unlocks the door and I collapse onto the passenger seat. "Can you give me a ride home? I live nearby."

Leo looks me over, taking in my ripped blouse and the bite marks on my neck. "What happened to you, Jolie? Did someone assault you?"

"Someone tried."

When Leo reaches for his radio, I swat his hand away. "Please don't report it. I was asking for trouble. I'm not myself right now. I let the wrong guy hit on me."

His features soften. "I heard about your brother, and I'm sorry. You're understandably going through a tough time. Are you sure you don't want to go after the bastard?"

"Positive. He got what he deserved. He won't be trying that again."

Leo furrows his brow. "Is the guy still alive?"

"He's in a lot of pain, but he's alive."

Leo puts the car in gear. "In that case, let's get you home."

I give him the address, and he speeds off. I study Leo's profile on the way. In the few years since I last saw him, he's gained a few pounds, and his hair is thinning on top. Middle age has set in. He's been patrolling Shockoe for as long as I've been around. "Have you ever considered doing something different, Leo?"

He glances over at me. "Nope. I love my job. I've passed up promotions several times. My wife is a research analyst for an investment firm. She earns the big bucks in our family. I'm making a difference on the streets. I'd be bored to tears in an administrative role."

My new job isn't as challenging as I'd hoped. Detectives follow up after a crime has been committed. Cops are on the scene when the action happens. I prefer to be in the thick of things.

When Leo drops me at the front of Jason's building, I say,

"Can we keep this between us? I don't want everyone worried about me. I'm doing fine, really. I just had an off night."

Pinching his fingers, he drags them across his lips. "Mum's the word. Call me if you ever need to talk. I was fifteen when my brother died in a drowning accident. I know what it's like to lose a sibling."

"I'm so sorry. I didn't know. I'd like to hear about him sometime. Thanks for the ride," I say, and slam the car door.

Inside the lobby, I glimpse myself in a mirror. I'm a mess with unkempt air, blood trickling down my neck, and a red cheek where Russell slapped me. I'm relieved not to encounter anyone in the elevator.

I take one of the sleeping pills Jason's doctor friend gave me and crawl into bed fully clothed. I sleep until past noon the next day. I open my eyes to the sight of my gun on the bedside table.

I let out a loud groan. I screwed up on so many levels last night. I know better than to take my gun out of the safe when I've been drinking. Even worse, that I left home in my condition with a loaded gun at my waist. My risky behavior jeopardized my safety and my career. The gun saved my life, but things could've been so much worse. Someone was looking out for me last night. *Jason* was looking out for me.

My head is pounding, my body aches, and I'm craving alcohol. I push myself up and sit on the edge of the bed until the room stops spinning. I spot a framed photograph of Jason and me on his chest of drawers. I traipse across the room and pick up the frame, running my finger over my brother's gloomy little face.

The picture was taken on our tenth birthday. Our favorite foster parents were getting a divorce, and we'd just been told we were being separated. Later that night, in the darkness of our shared bedroom, we made a plan to meet at The Alamo on our eighteenth birthday. I still remember Jason's words. *You're a survivor, Jolie. Be strong and fight for keeps.* He took my hand and placed it on his chest. *You will live in my heart until we meet again.*

The next day, our social worker found a foster couple willing to take both of us.

Returning the photograph to the chest, I shift my gaze heavenward. "You will live in my heart, Jason, until we meet again."

I go to the kitchen and pour every drop of tequila down the drain. After two cups of strong black coffee, I take a long hot shower and dab antibiotic ointment on the bite marks on my neck. Fortunately, the bites are far enough back on my neck for my hair to hide them.

I pick up a salad bowl from Roots Natural Kitchen on my way over to the cemetery. I haven't been here since the memorial service, and I'm pleased to see Jason's name etched in the granite plate on his niche. I sit down on a nearby park bench to eat the first substantial meal I've had since before Jason died. I carry on a one-sided conversation with my brother, telling him how badly I screwed up last night and how lost I feel without him. I imagine what he'd say if he were here. He would tell me that, in order to address the symptoms, I need to get to the root of the problem. The crippling anger and sadness are the problem. If only I could figure out how to control them. Drowning them with booze is only making matters worse. Jason was a proponent of physical exertion. I haven't exercised since before he died.

I dump my empty salad container into a trash can and hit the pavement, race-walking the winding streets of the cemetery. It's blazing hot, and I'm soon dripping with sweat. I can smell the tequila emitting from my pores. But it feels good to perspire, to cleanse my body of the impurities I've consumed over the past few days.

I walk for over two hours. I'm exhausted when I return to my truck, and my heart is still heavy, but I'm able to focus for the first time in days.

Back at home, I take another shower and dress in gray knit loungewear. I stretch out on the bed and fall into a deep, restful sleep. Jason is the first thought that enters my mind when I wake around dinnertime. The deep sorrow has returned, along with the temptation to drink. But there's no alcohol in the condo. And no food either.

I pad on bare feet into the kitchen and eat a spoonful of peanut butter. I make a cup of tea and power on my phone, thumbing through five days' worth of text messages from friends and coworkers. I don't respond to any, but their expressions of sympathy touch me deeply.

I listen to three urgent voice messages from Calvin, Captain Winnie, and Mel. They're worried about me and need to know I'm okay. I set the phone down. I'll call them tomorrow.

I open my laptop and sign onto the social media site with my largest following. Hundreds have posted thoughtful comments about my loss. How do they know?

I've only podcasted sporadically since my video of Laurence Riley went viral back in April. I haven't had any inspirational material to share. I drag an armchair over by the window, and position my laptop so the camera captures the sun setting over the river in the background. I click the Live button and begin to talk.

"Good evening. I'm speaking to you off the cuff and from my heart. As many of you know, I recently lost my brother. My twin. My better half. Thank you for your kind words. Your thoughts and concerns mean more to me than I can say. I had coffee with my brother the morning he died. He told me he was getting engaged and showed me the ring. If only I'd known that would be the last time I'd see him alive. There's so much I would've told him. So much I wanted him to know."

The number of viewers watching me rapidly ticks up, increasing from hundreds into the thousands.

"Jason and I never knew our father and were abandoned by our mother. We were six years old when she dropped us off at the police department in Amarillo, Texas. I would never have survived without Jason. He was my rock. I don't know *how* to live without him. I don't *want* to live without him. I'm struggling. I'm surrounded by darkness. I'm at the bottom of the ocean, gasping for breath. I can see the light at the top, but my pain has rendered me paralyzed. I'm trying, but I can't swim toward the surface."

"Many of you have experienced tragic loss. How did you survive?"

I read out loud the comments from my followers. "According to Sara, time is the only healer."

"Alex suggests I surround myself with friends and loved ones. Maybe one day, Alex. Right now, I just want to be alone."

"Christine's therapist really helped her. I see a lot of therapy in my future, Christine."

My breath hitches when I see the name of the next commenter. "Calvin writes: Jason was a hero, a modern-day Romeo. He risked his life to save the woman he loved. And you're a hero too, Jolie. You saved hundreds of people in the emergency room that day. And now you must save yourself. Your mission in life isn't over. You're only just beginning to make a difference. If you can't do it for yourself, do it for Jason. He's up there watching you."

I suck in an unsteady breath. "Thank you, Calvin. Thank all of you for the pep talk." A tear spills from my eye, and I wipe it away. "That's all for now. Thanks for joining in and for your support during these tough days."

I end the live segment and shut down my computer. I stand and turn toward the window, watching the sun dip below the horizon. Another long night is ahead of me, endless hours of loneliness and sleeplessness. The urge to drink is strong. I check my watch. I can make it to the liquor store before it closes. Retrieving my bag from the bedroom, I'm reaching for the doorknob when someone knocks. I freeze with my hand on the knob. I'm not in the mood for company.

More knocking is followed by Calvin's voice. "I know you're in there, Jolie. You have thirty seconds to open the door before I kick it down."

I'm busted. He saw my video. He knows I'm here. There's no putting him off this time. I open the door.

"You look like shit," he says.

"Gee thanks."

He gestures at my purse. "Are you headed out?"

"I am," I say, but I don't tell him where.

"Have you eaten dinner?"

"Yep," I say, unable to meet his gaze.

He folds his arms over his chest. "Oh, yeah? What'd you have?"

"Peanut butter."

He tilts his head to the side. "A peanut butter sandwich?"

"A spoonful."

He strides over to the refrigerator and opens the door. "There's nothing in here. Not even a bottle of ketchup."

I shrug. "I've been too busy to go to the grocery store."

"Busy doing what?"

I glare at him. "Mourning."

"Come on," he says, grabbing my hand. "I'm taking you out to dinner."

His grip is strong, and I lack the strength to resist.

Cool temperatures have replaced the heat from earlier, and a gentle breeze ruffles my hair when we exit the building. We walk in a companionable silence over to The Tobacco Company.

Calvin orders a Heineken in a bottle, and when I ask for sweet tea, he raises an eyebrow.

As soon as the waitress leaves, he says, "No tequila?"

I stare down at the table. "The tequila was becoming a problem."

"I figured as much," he says with a sigh. "Taking those first baby steps back into the real world is difficult, but the longer you wait, the harder it'll be."

"How am I supposed to walk when I'm barely crawling?"

"You can start by coming back to work. It won't be easy, but everyone at the department supports you."

"I'm not sure I'm coming back to work," I say and tell him my reservations about my new job.

"At least talk to Captain Winnie. Tell her your concerns. Your life needs purpose, Jolie. You can't stay holed up in your brother's condo with his ghost for the rest of your life."

The waitress returns with our beverages, and we order dinner—the meatloaf for Calvin and the crab cake for me.

Calvin waits for the waitress to leave before taking a long pull of his beer. "Speaking of Jason's condo, how long are you planning to live there?"

I pause a beat. I haven't really thought about my living arrangements. "I'm not sure. Jason's presence has a hold on me. And I'm not ready to let it go." I take a swig of tea, wishing it was tequila. "He left me a small savings account. I can stay indefinitely if I want. But it's Jason's home. Not mine. Just like my apartment is Lucas's home. He lived there before we were married, and most of the furniture belonged to him. I'm ready for a place of my own. I was saving up to move to a new apartment when . . ." My voice trails off.

"You don't need two homes. You should get rid of one."

"My lease isn't up until the end of August. Considering the circumstances, the building's manager may make an exception in my case. If I get my act together, I could be out of the apartment by the end of the month. There's no sense paying rent when I'm not living there."

"Thatta girl. Now you're thinking in the right direction. I'll help you move."

I scrunch up my face as I consider the work ahead of me. "What will I do with Lucas's furniture?"

"Hmm." Calvin drums his fingers on the table. "Why don't you have a yard sale?"

"That's actually a brilliant idea. I'll move my stuff to the condo and sell the rest. Surrounding myself with some of my things—my books and the rest of my clothes—might help Jason's condo feel more like home. Right now, I feel like a visitor."

"Agreed. And for God's sake, buy some groceries."

This tangible first step toward moving on with my life brightens my spirits. While we eat, we discuss the logistics of moving and having a yard sale.

"Thank you for dragging me out," I say to Calvin on the walk home. "I really needed a change of scenery."

"Yes, you did. Fair warning. I'm going to ride herd on you. To make certain you keep taking these baby steps."

"Fine. Just promise you won't bust down my door."

He chuckles. "We won't have a problem if you stay in touch."

When we reach my building, I give him a kiss on the cheek. "I will. I might even take you up on your offer to help me move."

"Anytime." With a final wave goodbye, Calvin gets in his car and speeds off. As I watch his taillights disappear around the corner, I think about how, not so long ago, I couldn't stand to be in the same room with Calvin. He's proven to be a good friend. Because of his own tragic loss, he knows exactly what I need.

I head up to the condo, feeling more like myself than I have since Jason died. I'm getting ready for bed when I notice my packet of birth control pills in my cosmetic case. I've been such a mess this past week, I neglected to take them. I shudder to think how close I came to having sex with Russell. I would've insisted he use a condom, but accidents happen. A memory comes crashing back to me. Calvin and me on the sofa hours after Jason died. He didn't use protection. Is it possible I got pregnant? Surely not. It was just a quickie. I shrug off my concern and drop the packet in the wastebasket. I won't be needing them. I've sworn off sex for the foreseeable future.

BACK ON PATROL

The dark cloud of grief hovers over me as I forge ahead with my life. The urge to drink is intense, but I keep my mind occupied and my body in motion. I pack up my meager belongings from my apartment, and on Sunday morning, Calvin helps me move my three most cherished items over to the condo. A leather-top Queen Anne desk I bought at the antique mall. A bookcase I found at a yard sale and lacquered navy blue. And a made-to-look-old Oriental rug in pale shades of gray and blue that I saved for months to buy.

We rearrange Jason's furniture to accommodate my stuff. I position the desk in front of the windows and the bookcase against his exposed brick wall. With the Oriental on the floor, the living room feels homier.

To show Calvin my appreciation for helping me move, I treat him to brunch at LuLu's. We devour every bite of the chicken and red velvet waffles. We're finishing our beverages—coffee for me and a Bloody Mary for him—when Calvin says, "Now that we've sorted your living situation, you can focus on figuring out your career."

I shake my head. "My living situation is far from sorted. I have the yard sale next Saturday. I need this week to get ready."

He blows air through his lips, letting out a puffing sound. "You're procrastinating. What do you have to do to get ready? Make a few signs, throw an ad up on Craigslist, and put stickers on the furniture left at your apartment. You can do all that in an afternoon. Which leaves you entirely too much free time to get into trouble."

By trouble, he means getting drunk.

Calvin eyes my phone on the table. "Text Winnie now. Meet with her tomorrow."

I hesitate, trying to think of a good excuse, but I don't have one. "I guess you're right. I can't put it off any longer." I thumb off a text to the captain. She responds immediately, summoning me to her office at eight tomorrow morning.

Calvin drains the last of his Bloody Mary and sets his glass down on the table. "Ready to hit the grocery store?"

I roll my eyes. I'm tired of him harassing me about stocking up on food. "I don't need an escort to the grocery store, Calvin."

"Yes, you do." He gets up and pulls me to my feet. "You won't go if I don't make you."

"Fine," I say, and let him drag me out to the parking lot.

I make out my grocery list on the drive to the Carytown Publix in Calvin's truck. Before Jason died, I fueled my body with healthy foods. I made myself dinner almost every night and packed my lunches for work. As Calvin pushes the cart through the produce section, I load up on fruits and vegetables. The routine of shopping for groceries makes the day seem almost normal. When I get to the floral section, I pick out an orchid and a potted plant for my new home.

Back at the condo, Calvin insists on helping me put away the groceries. But when he suggests we go for a walk, I say, "It's steaming hot out. I'd rather take a nap. I appreciate what you're trying to do, Calvin, but you can stop playing nanny to me. I'll be fine."

Calvin lets out a sigh. "All right. But only because I have my own errands to run. I'll check in with you later today."

I hold up my phone. "I'll be waiting with bated breath."

I walk Calvin to the door and lock it behind him.

I spend the afternoon arranging my clothes in the guest room closet. I'm not ready to clear out my brother's things. Jason's presence is the strongest in his room. I've been sleeping in his bed, where his scent still lingers on his pillows. And I'll continue to spend time there when I need to feel near him. But I'm claiming the guest room as my own, my first step toward breaking the strong bond that ties me to my brother's ghost.

CAPTAIN WINNIE IS on the phone when I arrive on Monday morning. She motions me to a chair opposite her desk. She talks a minute more before ending her call. Straightening, she returns the phone to its cradle.

"So, Jolie, how are you holding up?"

I lift a shoulder in a half shrug. "I'm hanging in there. Some days are better than others."

She places her hands, fingers entwined, on the desk. "Are you ready to come back to work?"

"Not exactly." I look away, unable to meet her gaze.

Irritation crosses her face. "Why are you here, then? Are you resigning?"

I let out a gush of air and lean forward in my chair. "Calvin suggested I talk to you, to express my concerns about the detective position. Even before Jason died, I was having hesitations. I miss the endorphin rush of being a first responder. Every shift is different. You never know what the day will bring."

Captain Winnie jabs a finger at me. "You should see your face right now. Your eyes are lit up like Yankee Stadium. So, you want to be a cop again."

I hesitate a beat. Once I make this admission, there's no turning back. "I'm *considering* it."

Captain Winnie stands abruptly. "Then we have a lot to discuss. I could use a coffee. Let's go across the street to Starbucks. I'm buying."

The captain grabs her purse, and we exit the building together. Over at Starbucks, she goes to the counter for our coffees while I snag a free table by the window.

Captain Winnie hands me a coffee and sits down across from me. "Let's back up a few years. Tell me, why'd you leave the department in the first place?"

I focus my attention on Winnie's hypnotic green eyes as I attempt to explain. "I felt like I was missing something. Like I was meant to be doing something more meaningful with my life. I have a lot to share with the world. And I'm still interested in being a journalist, but I learned the hard way, I can't make a living podcasting and freelance writing. I'm on a journey." I press my hand against my chest. "I feel it in my heart. Jason is guiding me. He's showing me the way. And I have to follow."

"Being a police officer is a meaningful occupation, Jolie. We save lives. We help the good folks and lock up the bad guys."

I lower my gaze to my coffee. "I realize that. Truthfully, Captain, if you're looking for a commitment, I'm not sure I can give it to you. I'm struggling with my grief. I need to work, to stay busy. I don't know what tomorrow will bring, let alone six months from now."

"I appreciate your honesty." Captain Winnie sits back in her chair. "You were a damn fine cop, Jolie. One of the best I've ever seen. I'm willing to give you a chance, hoping you'll make this your permanent career. When can you start? Is today too soon?"

A smile spreads across my face, and a warm feeling surges through my body. Until this second, I didn't know how much I wanted to return to the department. This feels right. Jason is watching over me. "Today is perfect. But I'd prefer to work nights."

Captain Winnie nods. "The lonely hours. I understand."

"But I need next Friday and Saturday off. I'm combining households, and I've committed to a yard sale."

The captain rises from the table. "That shouldn't be a problem. Let's go back to the station and you can work out the details with Lieutenant Gannon."

I practically skip alongside Winnie on the way across the street to the station. "Would it be possible for me to work toward a position with the tactical unit?"

"I think you're an ideal candidate for the SWAT team," the captain says, giving me the first glimmer of hope I've experienced in a very long time.

MY FIRST WEEK back is the hottest of the summer so far. The street thugs are on edge. We make many arrests every night, mostly drug possessions and drunk-and-disorderlies. I'm partnered up with Leo, and I'm grateful he doesn't mention driving me home after the attack. Our personalities are compatible. He's quiet by nature, and I'm not in the mood for idle chitchat. He's a seasoned cop. Instead of chastising me when I make mistakes, he's patient in explaining the proper way to follow procedure.

My days fall into a routine. I work from four in the afternoon until two in the morning. I manage a few hours of sleep before I'm inevitably awakened by a recurring nightmare from the day Jason died. I head out early for my version of boot camp—a long run followed by military-style calisthenics. After breakfast, I spend a few hours creating podcasts. Mentioning no names, I tell my listeners about the people and danger I encounter on the street. My content seems to resonate with them. As a result, my following grows.

Most days, I arrive at work early. I follow up with complaints citizens make through the nonemergency police hotline. On the first Wednesday of August, I read a report from a woman concerned about the sound of her neighbor's children crying. I disregard the report at first. Children cry. Dogs bark. But as I read further, my curiosity mounts. The woman, Linda Collins, claims she hears crying next door late at night, but she's never seen a child enter or exit the house during the day.

Instead of calling her, I get in my truck and drive to her house, which is in an undesirable neighborhood on the outskirts of the city. Linda comes to the door wearing a housecoat with her hair in curlers.

I flash my badge. "I'm Officer Jolene Hogan, following up on a complaint you made to our nonemergency hotline."

"Oh, right. I'm surprised you actually came." She steps onto her covered stoop, pulling her door closed behind her. "You must think I'm nuts complaining about crying children. But the man who rents the house next door doesn't have any kids. Or a wife."

"Are you sure the crying you heard was a child and not an adult?"

Linda plants a hand on her hip. "I'm positive. I can hear a pin drop. My late husband called me a bat. In case you didn't know, bats have exceptional hearing."

I scrunch up my face. "I *didn't* know that, actually."

Linda bobs her head. "They do. They rely on their hearing to survive." She gives me a skeptical look. "You know bats are blind, don't you?"

"I did know that. Hence the saying, blind as a bat."

"There's nothing wrong with my vision. And I'm telling you, I've never seen a child coming or going from that house."

I follow her arthritic finger to the ramshackle one-story house next door.

"But I hear those precious children sobbing their little hearts out at night. Just tears me to pieces inside." She grips my arm with surprising strength. "You gotta check it out, Officer. Something evil is going on inside that house. I'm sure of it."

I open my department-issued iPad and type a few notes. "You mentioned the house is rented. Do you know the owner?"

"His name is Clayton Murphy," she says and recites his phone number off the top of her head.

Furrowing my brow, I thumb the number into the iPad. "Are you related to Clayton?"

"Nah. But he's owned that house since I've been living here, going on thirty years. I call Clay at least once a week. The current tenant isn't taking care of the place. Look at the yard. It's a disgrace."

I glance over at the yard. The weeds are knee high. "How does Clay respond to your complaints?"

"He doesn't. He's avoiding me. But that doesn't stop me from calling. I leave messages all the time."

I snap the cover shut on the iPad. "Thank you for the information, Mrs. Collins. I'll see what I can find out."

Turning my back on her, I dismiss the woman as a meddling old busybody. But as I cross the street to my truck, an eerie feeling overcomes me. Am I being watched? Is there more to this story than meets the eye? I look heavenward. "Are you sending me a message?" I say out loud to Jason. "Is there something more going on here?"

I think about what I confessed to Captain Winnie over coffee. *I feel it in my gut. Jason is guiding me. He's showing me the way. I have to follow.*

On the way back to the station, I call Clayton Murphy. When he answers on the second ring, I introduce myself and explain why I'm calling.

Clayton's voice is gruff. "That old woman is batshit crazy, Officer. Don't listen to a word she says."

"What do you know about your tenant?"

"The only thing I need to know. He pays his bills on time. If you've gotta problem, take it up with him."

This doesn't sit well with me. "Aren't you worried your tenant is conducting illegal business in a property you own?"

"You're getting way ahead of yourself, little lady. Call me when you have evidence to back up that crazy bitch's story."

"I'll do that," I say, and end the call.

I spend the next two afternoons parked across the street in my truck, staking out the ramshackle house. Not a soul enters or leaves the dwelling. But I can't shake the feeling something sinister is taking place inside.

On Friday night, Leo and I are parked in Shockoe Slip, sipping strawberry cheesecake milkshakes from Cookout, when I tell him about my visit with Linda Collins and subsequent phone call with Clayton Murphy. "I agree with Clayton. The woman isn't playing with a full deck. But she was adamant about the crying. I can't explain it, but I have a gut feeling about this, Leo."

"And I've learned it's best not to ignore those kinds of feelings." Leo starts the engine. "Let's go have a look."

On the drive over to Linda's neighborhood, I confess I've done a little more digging into the current tenant's background. "Rodney Garza has only been renting the house a few months. Prior to that, a single mother and her teenage son lived there for four years. Best I can tell, Rodney Garza is in the country illegally."

Leo's jaw tightens. "I don't like the sound of that." He turns onto Linda's street and slows in front of her house. Lamps burn in her front living room window, but the house next door is pitch black. We idle on the curb for at least ten minutes. We're about to drive off when a flash of light from inside the house illuminates a child in the window with palms pressed against the glass.

Leo's head pivots toward me. "Did you see that?"

"Yep. Looked like a kid to me."

"Same. We're checking this out." He calls dispatch, reports our location, and asks for backup.

Leo and I approach the house with weapons drawn. He pounds on the door and calls out, "Police! Open up!"

The door opens a crack, revealing a brown eyeball. "Can I help you?"

"Are you Rodney Garza?" I ask.

"Who wants to know?" the man says.

Leo plants his foot in the way so Garza can't close the door. "We're Richmond City police officers, and we have some questions to ask you."

I hear muffled cries coming from within. "He's not alone," I whisper to Leo.

Leo barges into the door, knocking Garza off balance. When Garza stumbles backward, Leo goes after him while I clear the other rooms. In a tiny bedroom at the back of the house, I find at least forty children of very young ages and different ethnicities.

The kids' eyes are wide in fear, and they shrink back when I enter the room. Kneeling down, in a soft voice, I say, "It's okay. You can trust me. I'm the police. I'm here to help."

A little girl rushes me, knocking me onto my butt and crawling into my lap. Her arms are tight around my neck, and she's crying hysterically.

Leo enters the room. "What the hell?"

I get to my feet, holding tight to the little girl. She's as light as a feather, and I can feel her rib cage through her filthy dress.

Leo calls the patrol lieutenant on duty. "We have a child trafficking situation. Get the FBI over here now," he says and shouts out the address.

With the radio pressed to his ear, he asks me, "Can you handle things in here while I take care of Garza and wait for backup?"

"Of course." Dropping back to the floor, I sit cross-legged, letting these children crawl all over me. Some speak foreign languages. Some speak English. A few don't talk at all, their dazed expressions hinting at trauma that may have rendered them mute.

One little girl with haunted doe eyes says, "Hey, lady, will you help me find my mama?"

I kiss her greasy hair. "There are people on the way who will take good care of you. They will do everything they can to help you find your family."

My heart breaks for these innocent children. I can't imagine what they've been through. Where they've come from. The savagery they've endured. What would have become of them if we hadn't intervened?

I stay with them—stroking their hair, hugging them, wiping away their tears—until the FBI finally shows up.

When I emerge from the house, Captain Winnie is standing in the front yard with an attractive young woman wearing an FBI badge pinned to her belt. Winnie motions me over and introduces me to Tamara Hale.

The captain smacks me on the back. "Excellent work, Jolie. Leo tells me you stumbled upon this operation by following up on nonemergency leads."

My face warms. "That's correct." Surveying the property, I notice Linda Collins standing at the edge of the yard in the same housecoat she was wearing the other day. I wave at her. "That woman deserves the credit. She reported hearing children crying late at night but seeing no sign of them during the day."

Tamara says, "We've been investigating a large East Coast trafficking operation. We suspect this is a part of that. We've taken Garza in for questioning."

"Where did the kids come from?" I ask Tamara. "Were they kidnapped? Did their parents sell them?"

"Probably a mixture of both," she says.

I watch the FBI agents lead the children out of the house to a waiting van. "Where will you take them now?"

"To a nearby facility where they'll receive food and medical care," Tamara says. "We'll begin the process of reuniting them with their families."

"And what if you can't find their families?"

"They'll go into the foster care system or a children's home. More likely the latter, since the foster care system is stretched pretty thin right now." Tamara's expression is serious, a sign of how much she cares about these children.

Out of the corner of my eye, I see Calvin's unmarked car pull alongside the curb across the street. He notices me and hurries over. "I'm impressed, Jolie. First week on the job and you're busting a child trafficking ring."

I hold up two fingers. "Second week on the job. It was so awful, Calvin. All those poor little children." My emotions get the best of me, and I burst into tears. "I'm sorry."

"No worries." Tamara holds up her hand. "I get it. This is tough stuff. The atrocities children face these days is unfathomable."

"Come here." Calvin drags me off to the side. He puts his arms around me and holds me tight. I've grown accustomed to his embrace. His strength gives me courage. We're kindred spirits. We've both experienced tragic losses. He lowered his guard, allowed me to see his vulnerable side. The side he hides behind a wall from the rest of the world.

If only I could erect such a wall. If I could keep people at bay instead of letting them get close. Like these little children. I made the mistake of letting them inside my heart. Imagining what they've been through and the long road that lies ahead for them is incomprehensible. Their tear-streaked, dirty little faces have etched themselves into my mind.

I cry harder into Calvin's chest, and he whispers to me, "It's past two. You're officially off duty. I'll drive you back to the station for your truck." With one arm bracing me, he walks me to his car.

I stare out the window on the silent drive to headquarters. Calvin has slept with half the women in the department. I understand his sexual promiscuity better than most. That insatiable need that exists deep within my core, which sex satisfies for a brief few moments. Calvin and I are birds of a feather. We get each other. Is it possible there's more than friendship between us?

He pulls into the parking deck back at headquarters and parks in the empty spot next to my truck.

I place my palm on his cheek. "Thanks for rescuing me. I'm sorry I fell apart on you again."

Smiling, he kisses my wrist. "What're friends for?"

I lean across the console and press my lips to his. He jerks his head back, as though electrocuted. "Jolie . . . I . . ."

His reaction surprises and confuses me. I grab my bag and climb out of the truck. He doesn't call after me.

I drive home with tears blurring my vision. Seated at my desk, I open my laptop and click on my microphone. I talk about busting the trafficking ring, and I pour out my feelings for those children. My emotions are raw. My story will resonate with my listeners. When I'm finished, I turn off the microphone. I will edit the podcast before airing it later today.

With a heavy heart, I traipse down the hall to my bedroom. Calvin's emotional support has gotten me through these difficult past few weeks. I never would've survived without him. He gave me his friendship, and I betrayed him by hitting on him. I really screwed up. I crossed a line, and there's no going back. But as I lie in my bed, my mind drifts away from Calvin and back to the children. I imagine their arms around my neck, their trembling bodies pressed against mine. Jason led me to that ramshackle house. He's sending me a message. I have no clue what it means. But I know with absolute certainty, I'm about to find out.

GANG WAR

As the weeks of August wear on, I pour myself into my work. My emotions are a hot mess, but to everyone around me, I'm invincible. And I'm aggressive. Leo repeatedly warns me to take it easy when apprehending suspects. And I'm fearless. Not afraid of getting shot or killed. No one is waiting for me at home. But Jason is waiting for me in heaven when I die.

My nightmares worsen. Now, when I dream of Jason in the emergency room, he's surrounded by innocent children, the trafficking victims. In order to save them, I must take out the shooter. But when I fire my weapon, everyone goes down in a bloody massacre.

To avoid the nightmares, I sleep as little as possible. When Mel urges me to return to boot camp, I jump at the opportunity to fill those predawn hours. Instead of being strung out from lack of sleep, I channel that edginess into my workouts. I pressure myself into being the fastest and the strongest in my group.

Calvin ignores me at every turn. When I encounter him in the hallway at headquarters, he goes the other way. When I receive a commendation for helping bust the child trafficking ring, everyone in the department congratulates me except him. And he ignores my endless stream of texts. I apologize for making a pass at him. I tell him I miss our friendship. I send him funny memes. Nothing gets a response. I'm wounded and confused by his snubs. What I did isn't a crime. I tried to kiss him. I didn't kill his grandma. Maybe I misjudged him. Maybe the kindness he showed me after Jason died was only an illusion. But I know that's not true. The vulnerable Calvin—the one who opened up to me and let me see his soul—is the real Calvin. This egomaniac who struts around the department making passes at every pretty woman is a fraud. Calvin led me to believe we were friends, and then he ripped that friendship out from beneath me the first time he disapproved of something I did. I don't need friends like that.

I allow my hurt to morph into anger. Anger I can handle.

On Wednesday of the last full week in August, Mel invites me to go for a quick coffee after boot camp. "I have something I need to talk to you about."

We go to Urban Farmhouse on Cary Street in Shockoe Slip where we order bagels and coffee and split an order of fresh berries and melons. We grab a table by the window and chat for a few minutes about our workout.

Gnawing on her bagel, Mel says nonchalantly, "Did you know Calvin's seeing Brenda?"

The bottom falls out of my stomach, but I manage to keep a straight face. "Who's Brenda?" I ask, although I suspect she's the pretty blonde rookie with the shapely butt I saw Calvin leaving the station with the other night.

"She's the hot rookie all the guys have been drooling over."

"Good for Calvin," I say. "We should warn her about him."

Gulping down her chunk of bagel, Mel plants her hands on the table, fingers splayed. "Cut the crap, Jolie. I know you have a thing for him."

"Ha. What makes you say that?" I feign indifference as I sip my coffee.

"Calvin told me. He asked me to talk to you. He's worried you're upset about Brenda."

I choke and coffee shoots up my nose. "What an arrogant ass," I say, wiping my nose with a napkin.

Mel falls back in her chair. "Something's going on between the two of you. Don't deny it, Jolie. I know you too well."

I consider how much to tell her and decide honesty is the best policy. At least partial honesty. "Calvin was a good friend to me after Jason died. He lost his sister when he was in college, and he understood what I was going through. He drove me back to the station the night of the child trafficking raid. I gave him a quick kiss on the lips. It was a friendly gesture. But the jerk took it the wrong way. He hasn't spoken to me since."

"You can tell me the truth, Jolie. You wouldn't be the first woman to have her heart broken by Detective Casanova." Judging from her tight smile, Mel is one of those women.

"My heart is fine, thank you very much. I feel betrayed, because I thought Calvin was my friend. Not because I'm in love with him." I push back from the table. "Are you ready? You need to get to work, and I need a shower. I can't stand to smell myself anymore."

We gather our trash and throw it away on our way out the door. As we walk back to our cars, I ask, "Is it serious between Brenda and Calvin?"

"See!" Mel says, nudging me with her elbow. "You do have a thing for him. I knew it."

I give her a gentle shove in return. "I'm just curious."

"He's not in love with Brenda. I honestly thought he was in love with you." We arrive at our cars, and Mel clicks her doors unlocked. "What do you want me to tell Calvin?"

"Tell him the truth. I'm sorry he misunderstood my kiss. And that I'm seeing someone. I have been since before Jason died."

This is not true, of course. My relationship with Drew was in the budding phase. We'd been on the verge of a meaningful relationship when disaster struck, and my life went to hell. I've thought a lot about Drew these past weeks. I've picked up the phone dozens of times to call him. While I'm on the right path now, I don't trust myself enough yet to reach out to Drew.

Not until I've sorted my feelings for Calvin.

After showering, I spend the morning at my desk, editing my latest podcast. My following continues to grow on all social media platforms. My faith in humanity is restored, knowing blue lives still matter. When an email pops up in my inbox from a major advertiser interested in buying space on my podcast, I immediately respond and spend the next couple of hours setting up my first sponsorship.

I'm walking on air when I leave for work. I'm discovering my voice, and people are listening. Even the sight of Calvin and Brenda making out beside his truck in the parking garage doesn't bother me today. As I pass them, I yell, "Get a room." Childish, I know. But it gives me an extra kick in my step as I cross the street to headquarters.

The streets are quiet for a Wednesday night. Leo and I are parked at the bottom of Shockoe Slip when, across the radio, the dispatcher barks, "All available units! Reports of gunfire. Respond immediately." She follows up with the name of an apartment complex in Fairview Court, the most dangerous neighborhood in the city.

Leo speeds through the downtown streets to the interstate, where we join a convoy of squad cars with blue lights flashing. The dispatcher recites information about what appears to be a gang war. She instructs us to proceed with caution and notifies us the patrol lieutenant is on his way with riot gear.

The sound of rapid gunfire greets us as we approach the apartment complex. Leo adds our squad car to the line barricading the row of two-story outdated townhomes.

"Stay here," Leo orders. "I'll find out what's going on and get us some gear."

Swinging my door open, I crouch down beside the car, listening to the gang members screaming obscenities at one another.

A young woman sneaks up on me from the rear of the car. I don't hear her until she grabs ahold of my arm. "Help me! Please, dear God, you gotta help me!" She bounces from foot to foot, seemingly oblivious to the gunfire nearby.

I pull her down beside me. "Calm down and tell me what's going on."

"My daughter is alone in my apartment! You've gotta save her. Get her out now!"

The woman's dark eyes are wild, and she's clawing at her amber skin. I'm fairly certain she's on something. "How old is your daughter?"

She lowers her gaze. "She's three."

"Why would you leave a three-year-old alone?"

"I was next door at the neighbor's." She grabs a fistful of my uniform shirt and drags me to the rear of the car. "I live in the end unit. That one right there." Her arm shoots out, finger pointed to the end unit.

Peering over the trunk of the car, I follow her finger. Her apartment is at the opposite end of the row where the gunfire is taking place. Close enough for me to retrieve the child. "Are you sure she's alone?"

"I'm positive. She was sleeping when I left. Her bedroom is at the front, facing the street. You gotta get her out before them crazy bastards with the guns move this way," she says in a tone nearing hysteria.

"All right. But you stay right here. When my partner comes back, tell him where I've gone."

I unholster my gun and make a run for the apartment, not stopping to think about the rules I'm violating. The door is closed but unlocked. The living room is dark and quiet. I slide my way down the wall and up a flight of stairs. A night-light in the hallway provides a warm glow as I make my way to the front bedroom where the child is sitting up in bed, whimpering. She outstretches her arms to me. With the gun in my right hand, I scoop her up in my left arm. When I spin around to leave, a man steps from behind the door. A do-rag covers his head, and a large tattoo creeps up the left side of his neck to his face.

"Drop the gun or I'll shoot the kid." He trains a ghost gun at the little girl.

"Seriously? She's just a child."

He jabs his weapon at her. "I said drop the gun."

"Okay. Chill." I bend over, making like I'm going to set the gun on the floor and toss the kid onto the bed instead.

I raise my gun and we fire off shots at the same time. His bullet grazes my left arm. Mine hits him in the heart. He drops his weapon and stumbles backward into the wall. He slides down the wall to the ground, leaving a trail of blood behind him. Blood trickles from the corner of his mouth, and he stares blankly at me.

I hear footfalls on the stairs, and seconds later, Leo appears in the doorway. "What the fuck, Jolie? Are you crazy?"

He flashes his palm. "Don't answer that. Of course, you're crazy."

I pick up the screaming child, holding her tight. "Maybe. But I saved this kid."

"Let's get her outta here," he says, taking the toddler from me.

Hurrying down the stairs, we pause in the doorway to make

certain we're in the clear before darting across the pavement to our squad car. The woman snatches her child from Leo, thanking us repeatedly as she covers the little girl's face in kisses.

I open the back passenger door. "Get in and stay down. You'll be safe here. The car is basically bulletproof." I wait until they're inside before slamming the door.

Leo gives me the once-over. "Are you okay? Your arm is bleeding."

I glance down at my bloody shirt. "It's superficial. I'll live."

"Then let's get a move on."

We suit up in riot gear and join our coworkers gathered around a police van closer to the gunfire. When Captain Winnie gives the order, we approach the riot with full force. The war rages, ultimately leaving five gang members dead, dozens with gunshot wounds, and more than a hundred in handcuffs. A rookie, who took a bullet in the leg, is the only other cop who has been shot.

Rescue squads from all areas of the city arrive to transport the wounded to Richmond City Hospital. A paramedic friend fusses over me. "You need to get this looked at," he says, lifting my shirtsleeve to examine the wound.

"It's only a graze," I say, swatting away his hand.

"But it's deep. You need stitches." He motions me to the back of his ambulance. "Get in. I'll give you a ride."

"Thanks, but my partner can take me. Save your transport for someone more seriously injured."

Leo and I usher the woman and her child back to her apartment. Leo says to her, "Units will remain in the area overnight as a precautionary measure. If you need anything, don't hesitate to call for help."

I wag my finger at her. "Next time, don't leave your kid home alone."

"I won't," the woman says, hanging her head in shame.

Leo and I return to our squad car and head toward town. "Do you think the captain will fire me?" I ask.

"Nah. We're too short staffed." Leo smiles over at me. "You'll get a talking-to for sure. But I doubt you'll be suspended. After all, you saved the kid's life."

I think back over the events of the night. "What kind of mother puts her three-year-old's life in jeopardy? Women should have to pass proficiency tests before they're allowed to raise kids."

"Amen to that," Leo says under his breath.

The triage nurse at the hospital estimates the wait in hours. I shake my head. "Forget it. We'll come back another time."

"No way," Leo says. "Nasty infections come from bullet grazes. That needs to be taken care of tonight."

"Fine. I'll stay. But only if you go home. I can get an Uber."

Leo reluctantly agrees. "I'll get started on our report."

I find an empty seat in the corner of the crowded waiting room. This gang war is the worst riot Richmond has ever seen, and the 24-hour news networks are covering the story. I locate the TV remote and flip back and forth between the channels until a nurse calls me to an examining room.

I'm surprised when Stacy enters the room fifteen minutes later. I haven't seen her since a Sunday afternoon in late July when she came to the condo to claim her things. Jason's death is taking its toll on her, and she looks too thin and pasty.

"What're you doing here this late?" I ask.

"I heard about the riot, and I came to help." She lifts the sleeve of my hospital gown and examines the wound. "How did this happen?"

I tell her an abbreviated story about the child whose life I saved.

She doesn't comment. "You're going to need some stitches. Is there any chance you might be pregnant?"

My body goes still. "Why does that matter? It's a superficial wound."

She looks up at me. "It matters what type of pain meds I give you. *Is* there a chance you're pregnant, Jolie?"

My mind races. I didn't worry when I skipped my period. I'd stopped taking the pill, and I figured my cycle was all screwed up. "A slight chance, I guess."

Stacy lowers herself to the side of the bed. "When was your last period?"

"Um. In June sometime."

"Do you have any idea when you might've gotten pregnant?"

Without hesitation, I say, "On July thirteenth."

Stacy's mouth falls open. "The day Jason died."

I give her a somber nod. "After the shooting, a friend showed up at the condo to comfort me. He'd lost his sister in a car accident in college, and he understood what I was going through. I was out of my mind with grief. I had no clue what I was doing."

"So, he took advantage of your vulnerable state," Stacy says, her lips pressed into a thin line.

"Actually, I'm the one who took advantage of him. I practically raped him. It was over in a matter of seconds. I was in such a state of shock during those first few days, I completely forgot to take my pill."

"That was weeks ago. Forty-one days, to be exact. You need to know if you're pregnant, so you can make decisions. Do you want me to run a blood test? We'll have the results by the time I finish stitching you up."

Tears well in my eyes. "I guess."

Stacy places an arm around me. "Let's not get ahead of ourselves. The test might be negative."

Sniffling, I inhale a deep breath. "Right," I mumble, although the sick feeling in the pit of my stomach and the unexplained tenderness in my breasts I've been feeling lately tell me it won't be.

Stacy summons the nurse to draw blood, giving her rush orders for the lab. While she stitches up my wound, she tells me about her parents' new black Lab puppy. She tries to sound chipper for my sake. She knows I'm worried about the results of the pregnancy test. But her efforts are futile. She's no more cheerful than I am.

Once she stitches and bandages the wound, Stacy turns her attention to her laptop, her fingers flying across the keyboard. When her gaze shifts from the screen to me and back to the screen, I know she's received the lab results.

"You don't have to fake nice on my account, Stacy. I'm a big girl. I can handle the news. I'm pregnant, aren't I?"

"You are. Based on the date of conception, in a pregnancy timeline, you're eight weeks along."

"Great. I'm having a stellar year. First Lucas. Now Jason. Now this."

Stacy closes the laptop. "I'm ready to go home." She offers me a hand, pulling me up from the bed. "Come on. I'll give you a lift."

We walk to the parking deck in silence. The leather in her car smells new. Her Volvo SUV. Her mommy car. She was already planning her family with my brother.

"What're you going to do about the baby?" she asks when we're on the way.

I stare out the window as the first pink rays of dawn rise above the city's skyline. "I never wanted children. I'm not in a relationship with the father, and I can't see myself being a single mother. Not in my line of work, anyway. I don't really have much choice. I'll have to . . . you know, take care of it."

Stacy pulls to the curb in front of my building and takes the car out of gear. "Why don't you want children?"

My mother's words come back to me. *I never wanted to be a mother.* "I can't imagine bringing an innocent child into this cruel world. How much did Jason tell you about our childhood?"

Stacy shifts in her seat to face me. "Enough to understand why you're hesitant to have children. Jason felt the opposite. He wanted the chance to be a parent, to be the loving father he never had."

I let out a grunt. "Jason was the better half in our equation."

"That's not true. Jason talked about you all the time. He believed in you. He said you have much to offer the world, and you were only just getting started."

I think about the child I saved tonight and the child trafficking ring I helped bust. I can feel those children's tiny arms around my neck, clinging to me for dear life. "How can I make a difference in this world if I'm stuck at home with a baby?"

"This is the twenty-first century. You don't have to give up your career when you have a baby."

"I know." When I reach for the door handle, she grabs my arm.

"I'm here for you, Jolie, if you need to talk. This is a big decision. Take some time to think about it. Jason's presence is constantly with me. I feel him watching over my shoulder all the time. Knowing how close you two were, I'm sure you feel it too."

I nod, unable to speak for fear I might cry.

Stacy squeezes my arm. "You've heard the saying, 'When God closes a door, he opens a window.' I may be reading too much into this, but I don't think it's a coincidence your baby was conceived hours after your twin brother's death."

OPEN WINDOW

I wake from a gruesome nightmare covered in sweat. The dream rushes back to me. I'm in the emergency room. Jason is bleeding out on the floor in front of me. Children surround me, their tiny arms raised, begging me to pick them up. The shooter has his gun trained on my belly. My baby.

Last night's shocking revelation hits home. I'm pregnant with Calvin's baby. The man who can't stand to even look at me. Thank goodness I have the next two days off. I need time to make decisions and prepare for my inevitable meeting with Captain Winnie. She'll demand an explanation, and I'll tell her the truth. I don't regret breaking the rules to save that child. I'd do it all over again, even if it costs me my job.

I can't stop thinking about the feel of that child in my arms and the baby growing inside of my belly. Four months ago, I wouldn't hesitate to get rid of it. Is it possible what Stacy says is true about God closing a door and opening a window? What if Jason sent me this baby for a reason? Does he mean for me to give it to Stacy?

This concept takes seed and grows legs. By the time Stacy

calls to check on me late morning, I'm convinced this is what should happen, and I tell her as much.

Stacy sighs into the phone. "I've been thinking a lot about it. If you decide not to keep the baby, I'll definitely raise it as my own. Even though Jason isn't the father of your baby, you are his twin, which makes this child as much a part of him as I'll ever get. Besides, I'm a pediatrician. I'm a sucker for a baby."

"You're in a better position to raise the baby than me," I say. "Not only do doctors make way more money than cops, you have plenty of family in town to help you."

"Don't let the absence of family prevent you from keeping the baby, Jolie. I will be the doting aunt."

"That means a lot, Stacy. You're a wonderful person. I understand why my brother loved you so much." My breath hitches, and I croak out a goodbye.

A thought occurs to me as I end the call. There will come a point in Stacy's life when she's ready to move on from Jason's death. She'll meet someone new and start a life with him. How will my baby fit in? And how will I feel watching another woman raising *my* child? Giving the baby to Stacy has too many complications to be a viable option. A desperation I've never felt before brings on a torrent of tears. I'm tired of crying. I cry now for no apparent reason. Then I realize that some of these emotions may be related to pregnancy hormones.

An hour later, I'm eating a salad at the kitchen island when someone bangs on my door. My pulse quickens. Is it Calvin? Did he somehow find out about the baby? I tell myself that's impossible. Only two people know I'm pregnant—Stacy and me. When the banging continues, I slide off the barstool and cross the room to the door.

I'm stunned to see Drew standing in the hallway. He looks adorable in khaki shorts and a polo shirt. Despite the fluttering in my chest, I'm not in the right frame of mind to talk to him. "Now is not a good time," I say in a deadpan tone.

He jams his Allbirds sneaker against the door so I can't close it. "Please, Jolie. I went to a lot of trouble to get your address."

I tilt my head to the side. "How *did* you get my address?"

"I went to the police department. I refused to leave until they told me where you're living. Your friend Mel took pity on me. Just tell me why you've been avoiding me. Then, I'll leave."

"You wanna know why I've been avoiding you." Taking a step back, I hold my hands out by my side. "Look at me. I'm a mess. You deserve better than this, Drew. You deserve my best self, but I can't give that to you right now. I'm trying to figure out my life. And it's not going very well. With every three steps I take forward, I take two backward."

"Although we were just getting to know each other, we had something special. I felt it. And I think you did too." Drew's hangdog expression tugs at my heartstrings. "If you think we have a chance, I'm willing to wait as long as it takes."

I pinch the bridge of my nose, willing the tears to hold back. "I can't ask you to do that. It's not fair."

"Let me worry about what's fair. I've never met anyone like you, Jolie. You're special. You deserve a man who treats you like the rare gem you are."

From anyone else, the line would sound corny. But I know Drew means it. His sincerity causes the tears to flow. He takes me in his arms, and I bury my face in his chest. I think back to the day Jason died. I had dinner plans with Drew that night. We were finally going to make love. During the days prior, we'd teased each other into a sexual frenzy with our naughty texts and phone calls. That chemistry between us still exists. But there's something else between us. Something I haven't noticed before. I have the oddest sensation this is where I belong. I've finally come home after a long journey.

I lift my head and push him away. "I need a little more time, Drew."

He smiles down at me, his blue eyes twinkling. "And I'm fine with that as long as you respond to my texts. I won't blow up your phone. I'll just check in periodically to make sure you're okay."

"I promise I'll respond." I kiss his cheek. "You're a good guy, Drew. I won't string you along."

Drew turns toward the elevator, and I watch him disappear inside. Closing the door, I move to the sofa and stare out the window at the cloudy day. September first is less than a week away. The days are already shorter. An autumn chill will soon be in the air. I'll spend my first Thanksgiving and Christmas without Jason. I imagine the long winter nights alone in this condo with only my swollen belly to keep me company. My unborn baby. The child I never wanted to have. *I never wanted to be a mother*—the only lesson I ever learned from my mother.

I made a mistake. Why should I spend the rest of my life paying for it? Why give up a career I enjoy and a man who makes me happy? In my defense, I wasn't in my right mind when this baby was conceived. To hell with Stacy's closed-door-open-window theory. I need to get a grip, stop looking for signs from Jason. He isn't guiding me. He didn't plant this seed in my womb. He's playing golf in heaven, and I am down here facing life's challenges alone.

I jump to my feet and grab my laptop off my desk. I search for the nearest Planned Parenthood location and schedule an appointment for first thing tomorrow morning.

EAGER TO PUT this episode behind me, I arrive at Planned Parenthood early for my appointment the next day. The nurse who greets me is an older woman with a clipped tone and smug smile. "You'll need to speak with a counselor before the procedure," she says.

"Nothing anyone can say will make me change my mind. I just want to get this over with."

She hands me a clipboard with several forms attached. "Fill these out. One is a waiver stating you declined counseling."

"Fine," I say, snatching the clipboard from her.

Once the forms are complete, she shows me to an examining room and gives me a hospital gown. I change out of my clothes and sit down on the bed. The doctor enters the room, followed closely by the nurse.

He's an elf of a man with a bulbous nose and thick glasses. He explains the procedure and orders me to lie down. I plant my feet in the stirrups and close my eyes. Jason's image flashes before me, and his voice rings out in my head. *Don't do it, Jolie. You're a survivor. Be strong and fight for keeps.*

I clamp my legs together and sit up straight. "I can't do this!"

The doctor shrugs and leaves the room without another word. The nurse says, "You should've talked to the counselor. Would've saved us all some time."

On the way back to the condo, I stop at the grocery store for a gallon of salted caramel ice cream. If ever there was a time for comfort food, this is it. Perched on a barstool, I spoon ice cream straight out of the container. I don't feel guilty about splurging. If I'm gonna get fat, I might as well enjoy it.

I need to break the news of my pregnancy to several key people. And I know a way to tell them all at once.

Placing the ice cream carton in the freezer, I sit down at my desk, open my laptop, and turn on my microphone. Going live on my social media platform takes away my option to edit the content before posting. I've made my decision. This guarantees I won't change my mind.

As I recount the events of the previous forty-eight hours, the number of listeners ticks into the thousands and then tens of thousands. I briefly describe the gang war, saving the child, and the bullet wound that sent me to the hospital where I learned I was pregnant.

"In my darkest hour, I turned to a friend for comfort. The child's paternity isn't in doubt. I wasn't with anyone else before, and I haven't been with anyone since. I'm not in a relationship with the baby's daddy, and I expect nothing from him. It won't be easy, but I am determined to go it alone. Although I won't be alone in spirit."

I take the microphone in hand and lean back in my chair. "Those of you who have lost loved ones in the past will understand this better than others. Since my brother's death, I've sensed him watching over me, guiding me. He was with me the night I busted the child trafficking ring, and he was with me last night when I saved the little girl in the gang war. Yesterday, I convinced myself this was a ridiculous notion. There's no such thing as guardian angels. I scheduled an appointment for an abortion, but when I got to the clinic this morning, I couldn't go through with it. I felt Jason's presence greater than ever before."

I pause a beat to catch my breath. "Jason and I grew up in foster care. On our tenth birthday, we were told we were being separated. We made a plan to meet at The Alamo on our eighteenth birthday. Jason said to me, 'You're a survivor, Jolie. Be strong and fight for keeps.' Fortunately, our social worker performed a miracle so we could stay together. But those are the words that ran through my head this morning, in the minutes before I nearly ended my baby's life. I am a survivor, and I am strong, and I will fight to keep my child no matter the cost."

I straighten my chair and return the microphone to the desk. "Like a wise woman recently reminded me, when God closes a door, he opens a window. Jason's life is over, but a new life is just beginning. I will cherish this life, just as I cherished my brother.

"The time has come for me to face my new reality. I'm moving on with my life on my own terms. What does this mean for my career as a police officer? I won't risk my child's life by remaining on patrol. I haven't spoken with my captain yet, but I'm optimistic she'll allow me to work a desk job until the baby comes. As for my podcast, I'm not going anywhere. I hope you won't either. I've worked hard to establish a following, and I won't let you down. I have an idea for future content, and I think you'll like this new direction. Stay tuned in the days ahead for more information."

I glance at the computer's clock. I've been talking for nearly an hour. "That's all for now. Until we meet again, here's wishing you Godspeed in all your endeavors."

I end the live chat and turn off the microphone. When my phone blows up with texts, I power it off. I'm not ready to face those closest to me. Calvin's wrath. Drew's hurt. Mel's interrogation. But I spend hours responding to the online comments from strangers. Their support is overwhelming. Their kind words comfort me, and I keep the tissue box nearby. My Patreon membership doubles and triples, and the money rolls in.

Around nine o'clock, I crawl into bed and fall into a deep and dreamless sleep. I wake after eight o'clock the following morning feeling rested and more like myself than I've felt in weeks.

I SUMMON the nerve to power on my phone over a cup of herbal tea the following morning. No more coffee for me. I have many voice and text messages, but only three are noteworthy. A voice message from Captain Winnie, ordering me to get down to headquarters first thing this morning. A text from Stacy, saying she's proud of me for making the right decision and she'll be by my side until the child goes to college. And a text from Drew. *If only you'd trusted me.* There's no word from Calvin. Based on the way he's been behaving lately, I'm not surprised.

I expect a lecture from Captain Winnie. Instead, she embraces me in a bear hug and congratulates me. "I realize you didn't plan for this, but it will change your life and you will love this baby to pieces. You can count on me to help you in any way."

"Thank you for being so kind and understanding," I say. "I realize I've only been on patrol a few weeks, but I'd like to be transferred to a desk job until the baby comes."

"Of course. On the day shift, so you can get plenty of sleep at night."

I FIND DESK DUTY UNINSPIRING, and do my real work at night, networking with cops in nearly every major metropolitan city across the country. As a result, on the Tuesday evening after Labor Day, I interview the first guest on my podcast. Kathleen Griffin is a beat officer from Chicago who recently busted a crack house. She rescued a six-month-old baby, the child of an addict. A crack baby. Kathleen, the mother of two teenagers, has taken the child in and is petitioning for adoption. I break into tears when she talks about the medical challenges the child might face in its future.

My audience loves her. At the suggestion of one of my listeners, we set up a GoFundMe account, which raises tens of thousands of dollars for Kathleen and her baby.

My podcast—now titled *Inside the Lives of the Men and Women in Blue*—is an overnight success. My inbox is flooded with cops sharing their stories and hoping to get an interview. While I'm no longer patrolling the streets, I'm making a difference. I'm spreading the word about the impact cops are making in America.

I call Drew dozens of times. When he doesn't answer, I leave rambling messages, asking for a chance to explain. His silence is payback for all the weeks I ignored his texts and calls.

I see Calvin nearly every day at headquarters. He doesn't speak to me, but I feel his eyes on me, lingering on my thickening midsection—my developing baby bump.

Stacy hooks me up with a colleague who's an obstetrician. I have to wait two weeks for an appointment with Dr. Debra Reid, and when I go for my first checkup in mid-September, I hear the baby's heartbeat. The sound of a living being growing inside of me profoundly affects me. God has entrusted me with this child's care. I'm responsible for raising this baby from infancy until adulthood. That responsibility weighs heavily on me. I will never, under any circumstances, do to my child what my mother did to me.

Stacy and I text back and forth nearly every day, but in late September, we finally find time to meet for dinner at Cocadilla, the new upscale Mexican restaurant on Grove Avenue. A cold front has ushered in the first taste of autumn, and we request a table outside near the fireplace.

I study Stacy across the table, and I'm encouraged to see that life has returned to her warm brown eyes.

"You look good," I tell her. "What gives?"

Her lips curl into a smile. "I've been invited to join what I deem to be the best pediatric practice in the city."

"That's outstanding, Stacy! Congratulations," I say, offering her a high five.

The server brings our drinks—a margarita for Stacy and a limeade for me. Stacy takes a sip of her margarita and puts down her glass. Tilting her head to the side, studying me, she says, "Why do I get the feeling you want to talk to me about something?"

"How can you tell?" I ask, stirring my limeade with my straw.

"Your brow pinches right here," Stacy says, touching her forehead between her eyebrows. "Just like Jason's used to do."

The mention of my brother brings a smile to my face instead of tears to my eyes. While I'm saddened to be moving on with my life, for the baby's sake, I have to look toward the future.

"Actually, a number of your facial expressions remind me of him," Stacy says.

"Really? That's interesting. I never saw much of a resemblance between us. I can't wait to see if this baby looks like either or both of us."

A faraway look settles on Stacy's face. "Me either."

I fold my arms on the table. "But you're right. I do need to talk to you about something important. I'm planning to return to patrol when my maternity leave is over. Because of the danger associated with the job, I have to make plans for the baby in the event something happens to me. With no family of my own, I was wondering if you would consider adopting my child if I were to die."

"I'd be honored," Stacy says without hesitation. If she were anyone else, I'd worry about her hasty response. As a pediatrician, Stacy knows what she's getting into.

I give her hand a squeeze. "Thank you. That's a load off my mind."

The server brings our chips and guacamole, and we place our order for the main course.

"I'd like to make our agreement official," I say when the server leaves. "If it's okay with you, I'll have Jason's attorney friend, Chris, draw up a legal document."

"That's smart thinking." Stacy dips a nacho into the

guacamole. "You haven't told me much about the baby's father, except to say you're not in a relationship with him. If I'm to be the baby's guardian in the event something happens to you, I should probably know a little more about the father. Does he know you're pregnant?"

"He knows. If he didn't hear my podcast, he heard *about* my podcast. I see him nearly every day, and he hasn't said a word to me about the baby. Which I take to mean he's not interested."

"His *interest* in the baby doesn't matter. He's the biological father. He's equally responsible."

I shake my head. "Not really. I told you, I practically raped him."

"Puh-lease! You were in distress at the time. He could've stopped himself. But he didn't. If you ask me, he took advantage of you."

She makes an interesting point that I haven't thought of. "Maybe."

"You should talk to him, Jolie. At least find out if he ever plans to be a part of the child's life."

I promise Stacy I'll think about it, and over the course of the next few days, I think of little else. I conclude I don't want Calvin Ingram in my child's life. He has too many issues to be a positive role model. But Stacy is right about one thing. I need to clear the air with Calvin so we're on the same page about expectations.

After work on the following Wednesday, the first week in October, I find Calvin waiting for me outside the main entrance at headquarters.

"Jolie, we need to talk." I let him lead me out of the stream of people entering and exiting the building. "Am I your baby's father?"

"I assume you saw my podcast," I say, and he nods. "Then you know you're the father. You also know I don't consider this baby a mistake. This baby is a gift from God. Or Jason. Or both.

My baby is better off without you as its biological father, which means you're off the hook. Have a nice life, Calvin."

I take off across the street, but he catches up with me. "Jolie, wait!"

I glare at him. "What do you want, Calvin?"

"I don't know. To talk. To make sure you're okay."

"I'm fine and dandy. Look, I'll never forget your kindness during the weeks after Jason died. But I'll also never forget how quickly you turned on me when I tried to kiss you after the child trafficking bust."

A smirk tugs at his lips. "Why did you kiss me?"

"I've asked myself that a million times. I've yet to come up with an answer. I acted on impulse. Maybe I wanted to have sex with you. Maybe I was expressing my gratitude for your support during a tough time. Maybe I was simply an emotional wreck and needed comforting. Regardless of the reason for my behavior, you could've just told me you weren't into me. You didn't have to sever our friendship. You turned out to be the jerk I always thought you were."

I turn my back on him and run up the stairs of the parking garage. I'm almost at my truck when I hear footfalls behind me. I spin on my heels, expecting to see Calvin. "Leave—"

I'm dumbstruck at the sight of the woman standing in front of me. Something about her is eerily familiar. She's stunningly beautiful, with golden hair and dazzling blue eyes. *Jason's eyes.*

REVENGE

I stare agape at the woman who gave birth to me and took care of me for the first six years of my life. She's as familiar to me as she is a stranger.

Her lips part in a soft smile. "I'm your mother, Jolene."

My name on her lips brings back a fuzzy memory of her hovering over me. She's either giving me a bath or tucking me into bed at night. Whichever it is feels cozy.

She reaches for my hand, and I jerk it away. "I don't have a mother."

"You don't remember." Her tone is disappointed, as though hoping I'd remember but suspecting I wouldn't.

"I remember my mother dropping me off at the police department in Amarillo. I even remember what she said to me about never wanting to be a mother. That woman's been dead to me since that day."

"I had no choice, Jolene. I couldn't take care of you. I could no longer keep you safe." She glances around at the busy parking deck, at police officers coming and going from their shifts. "Is there somewhere we can talk? I'd like to explain."

I scrutinize her. She's tall and slender with shoulder-length hair cut in layers. She's dressed stylishly in designer jeans, a crisp white blouse, and seriously cute camel suede booties. She doesn't bear the appearance of a woman who's led a hard life. There are no deep lines etched in her face, and her teeth show no signs of decay from smoking meth.

"No thanks. I'm not interested in anything you have to say." I unlock my truck and climb behind the wheel.

She grabs the door so I can't close it. "I realize I've caught you off guard." She presses a folded piece of paper in my hand. "Call me when you're ready to talk." She turns and walks away.

My head spins with conflicting emotions as I watch her go. I can't process them at once. I drive over to Hollywood Cemetery and park near the Palmer Chapel Mausoleum. There is no one around, which I find hard to believe on such a crisp autumn day. I stand at the edge of an overlook, staring out across the river. After decades of feeling angry and hurt and betrayed, I'm surprised at how calm I feel. But I have so many questions.

My mother's words—*I could no longer keep you safe*—puzzle me. Keep me safe from what? Over the years, I've imagined many plausible reasons she would have abandoned us. Drug addiction. Poverty. Terminal illness. Incarceration for prostitution or bank robbery. A man. Is that it? Was there an abusive man in her life she couldn't get away from? Was that abusive man my father?

My mother said, "Call me when you're ready to talk." Not *if* but *when*. She's awfully sure of herself, which irritates the hell out of me. But how can I turn down the chance to get the answers I've so desperately needed for so many years?

My phone alarm goes off, reminding me of my scheduled podcast interview in an hour. Brad Price has been all over headline news in recent days after a cop-related shooting. He's agreed to tell his story to my viewers, and I don't want to miss it.

I hurry home, forcing my mother from my thoughts.

I spend the next few hours interviewing, editing, and posting my podcast. I'm exhausted when I finally turn in, but I can't sleep for thinking about my mother. And I call her on my way to work the next morning. She answers on the first ring. She sounds chipper, as though she's been awake for hours.

"Meet me tonight at six o'clock on Brown's Island at the base of the T. Pott. footbridge. I'm agreeing to hear you out. Nothing else," I say and hang up without waiting for her response.

An outdoor public place seems impersonal and safe. I can keep my distance and get away in a hurry if I need to escape.

The day drags on endlessly. I make long lists of questions, preparing for my mother's interrogation like an officer determined to nail her suspect. This may be my only opportunity, and I want to make certain I get all the answers.

I stop by home and change into leggings and a long-sleeve knit shirt on my way to meet my mother. She's waiting on a park bench at the designated spot when I arrive. She stands to greet me. She's wearing designer jeans again and a pale gray wrap sweater that looks expensive. Large sunglasses hide her eyes, and a large sunhat covers her golden hair. Around her neck, a cross charm dangles from a thin chain. For some reason, this surprises me. I don't remember her being religious. Then again, I remember so little about her.

Removing her sunglasses, her eyes travel my body, landing on my baby bump. "You're due in early April," she says, a statement not a question.

I place my hand on my belly. "How did you know?"

"I've listened to every one of your podcasts."

Which means she knows about Jason. I gesture at the footbridge. "Let's walk."

We cross to the center of the bridge, stopping at a lookout. "Start talking," I say in my most threatening cop's voice. "I've waited a long time to hear why you abandoned Jason and me."

She angles her body toward me. "Do you remember anything about your father?"

"Nope. Nada."

She draws in an unsteady breath. "Your father is a powerful man in Texas. His wife was the daughter of a Texas oil billionaire."

She lets this sink in. She was having an affair with a married man. Jason and I were born out of wedlock. "Go on," I say, staring down as the rapidly flowing water of the James River crashes against the rocks.

"He was miserable with his wife, but he refused to leave her because of the money. When I found out I was pregnant, he demanded I have an abortion. He was furious when I insisted on seeing the pregnancy through. You remember what I told you in Amarillo about never wanting to be a mother. But you don't remember all of it. I also said you and Jason were the greatest surprise, the most wonderful blessings, of my life."

My mother turns her back to the river and leans against the railing. "The abuse started after you and Jason were born. After the third visit to the emergency room, I threatened to take my documented evidence of our affair and his abuse to the press."

"Is he a politician or something?"

She nods. "A long-term senator with people on his payroll willing to do anything he asks. Shortly after I made the threat, your father's goons paid me a visit. They ransacked the apartment, looking for the documents, which fortunately I had stashed in a safe deposit box. They beat me within an inch of my life. When they finished, they gave me a message from your father. If I didn't keep my mouth shut, next time he would go after the kids."

Her chin quivers, and my hardened heart softens a bit. I've been involved in enough domestic violence cases to understand the brutality she must have endured.

When my mother pushes off the railing and starts walking, I step in line beside her. The sun is beginning its descent below the horizon, and I shield my eyes against the glare. "Did you call the police?" I ask.

"I was too afraid, too scared even to go to the hospital. A friend took care of you and Jason while nursing me back to health. She's the one who convinced me to go on the run. I had no money, and no way to support a family. I knew your father would never stop looking for me. And I knew if he ever found me, he would kill me. And I couldn't let you get caught in the crossfire."

We reach the opposite side of the bridge and turn back around. "I was on the run for twelve years," she says. "I would get settled somewhere, and a few months later, your father's goons would show up. I worked odd jobs, mostly waitressing. I was miserable without you and Jason, and I read romance novels to fill the long, lonely hours. I decided to try my hand at writing. By the time I found someone to counterfeit my new identity, I'd written a dozen novels. I published them all at once and became something of a success."

I stop dead in my track in the middle of the bridge. "Wait a minute. This sounds familiar. I remember reading about the mysterious, reclusive romance novelist in the news. Are you Clara Thomas?"

"In my heart, I will always be Sonya Hogan. But yes, I go by Clara Thomas now."

"Are you still in danger?"

"I've evaded your father for the past ten years. I live in a tiny town in Vermont. I feel safe there." She chuckles. "I even let my hair return to its natural color."

We reach the park bench and sit down side by side. "I made a friend at social services in Amarillo, Eileen Brady. She took extra special care of you. I kept tabs on you through her."

My eyes go wide. "We loved Miss Eileen. She spared us from being separated."

"That's right. The Cunninghams were her personal friends. They'd never been foster parents before, but Eileen convinced them to take you in. They were so proud when Jason got accepted into premed at VCU. And they were especially proud of your willingness to support him through school. If not for you, Jason would never have become a doctor."

Silence falls over us. A young woman and her daughter stroll past. The girl is talking animatedly about an incident that happened at school. When they reach the bridge, the mother takes her daughter's hand, and they head off with arms swinging. The child is about ten years old, the same age as I was when I went to live with the Cunninghams. They were kind people and good providers. But they lived by strict rules and showed little affection.

Heat flushes through my body. "All these years, you knew where we were, but we didn't know if you were even alive. Why didn't you reach out sooner?"

She fingers the gold cross charm on her neck. "I wanted to. Every single day of the past twenty-four years." She lets out a sigh. "Despite his threat, I never worried your father would hurt you or Jason. He loved you, as much as a psychopath can love anyone. And he was too much of an egomaniac to harm his offspring. But I know he's keeping tabs on you. For me to reach out to you would be walking into a trap."

"Hence the dark glasses and sunhat. What changed your mind? Why did you decide to come now?"

"When I heard about Jason . . ." Her voice trails off and tears well in her blue eyes. "I missed the opportunity to know my son. His death made me realize how precarious life is. I couldn't risk missing out on the chance to know my daughter."

I jump to my feet. "I agreed to hear you out. That's as far as it goes for now."

She stands to face me. "I realize that, Jolene."

"I go by Jolie now," I snap.

She smiles. "Jolie. It suits you." She places a hand on my face. Her soft touch brings back flashes of memories I can't string together. "I'm so sorry for your loss. I know how much you loved your brother. He was lucky to have you. When the two of you were little, you fussed over him like a mother hen. You've done the same as an adult, putting him through medical school and risking your life for him."

"Jason and I took care of each other. He lost his life trying to save the woman he was planning to marry."

She gasps. "I didn't know."

I stare down at the ground. "Jason invited me for coffee the morning he died. He showed me the engagement ring. Stacy's a wonderful person. A pediatrician. She would've been a loving wife." I look back up at her. "This is a lot for me to process. How long are you in town for?"

"The length of my stay depends on you, Jolie. I'll move here tomorrow if you're willing to give our relationship a chance."

Is it possible for us to have a relationship? I honestly don't know. "I can't make any promises. I have a lot to sort out."

"I understand. I'll at least be here through the weekend. I'd love to talk some more. Can I take you to dinner tomorrow night?"

"I'll think about it."

I turn my back, leaving her standing alone beside the park bench. A wave of guilt overcomes me as I return to my truck. She's been alone most of her life because of Jason and me. She sacrificed her happiness for our safety.

I start the engine, but I don't put the truck in gear. I'm confused, and I desperately need to talk to someone. I view this as a good sign, an indication that I'm finally getting my act together. The old me would've sought comfort in reckless ways. The new me wants to open up about my feelings. If only Drew were speaking to me . . . I miss the way he focuses his blue eyes on me, as though no one else in the world exists.

A wave of sorrow overcomes me. Jason is the person I need most right now. He's the only one who could understand what I'm going through. If I can't have Jason, I can have the next best thing. I click on Stacy's number. When she answers, I blurt, "Something's happened. I need to talk. Are you free?"

"Of course. I'm staying with my parents. I'll text you the address."

Ten minutes later, Stacy's mother greets me at the door in gray flannel pants and a lavender sweater set with a double strand of gray pearls around her neck. Marjorie gives me a warm embrace and then holds me at arm's length. "Look at you. You're adorable with your baby bump. Stacy and I want to throw a shower for you when we get closer to your date."

"Thank you," I say, forcing a smile. I'm not really the shower type.

Marjorie closes the front door behind me. "Stacy just got home from work. She's upstairs changing. She'll be down soon."

I follow Marjorie down the center hallway and through a set of French doors to the flagstone terrace where flames lick from the top of a gas fire pit. "Can I get you something to drink while you wait?"

Tequila on the rocks would be awesome right about now, but I say, "I'm fine, thank you."

"How about some herbal tea?"

I smile. "Herbal tea would be nice."

Four wicker lounge chairs surround the fire pit. I plop down in the one nearest me with my back to the house. I'm replaying my conversation with my mother when Stacy emerges from the house with two mugs of tea.

Handing me a mug, she sits down in the chair next to me. "This is a surprise."

"Thanks for letting me barge in. Are you living here now?"

"Temporarily. My apartment was too lonely without Jason. Once I settle into the new practice, I'm going to buy a house. For now, I really need to be with my family." She grips my arm. "I'm sorry. That was inconsiderate of me."

"Actually, family is the reason I'm here. My mother showed up out of the blue yesterday."

"No way! That's amazing. Jason was convinced she was dead. He was certain you would've heard from her otherwise."

I shake my head. "Jason and I were never on the same page about our mother. Whenever we talked about her, we ended up arguing. So, we avoided the subject."

Stacy sits back in her chair and crosses her legs. "Tell me everything. Where has she been all this time?"

I repeat what my mother told me earlier about her abusive relationship with my father, being forced to put us in foster care to keep us safe, and living on the run. "All these years, I've been so angry at her for abandoning us. Turns out I was angry at the wrong person."

"What's she like?"

I hesitate, deciding how best to describe my mother. "She looks like Jason, with golden hair and blue eyes. Come to think of it, she acts like him too. She has his gentle manner. You'll probably cry when you meet her." The words spill from my mouth before I can stop them. They are proof that I'm considering a relationship with my mother.

Stacy's eyes glisten with unshed tears. "Probably. Jason always hoped she'd come back into his life. He wanted to search for her. He even ordered a DNA kit, although he never sent in his sample."

A pang of envy grips my chest. Jason said nothing to me. But that's my fault for refusing to talk about her. "Did I mention she's a romance author? She goes by the name Clara Thomas."

Stacy taps her chin as she ponders the name. "Never heard of her."

I laugh. "I'm not surprised. I don't imagine you read too many romance novels."

She pops my arm with the back of the hand. "Hey! I resent that. I like to read. I just prefer mysteries."

"And literary novels with complicated plots and flowery description."

"No thanks. If I'm not hooked in the first chapter, I won't continue to the second."

"I heard that." I push myself up out of the chair. "I've gotta go."

Stacy stands. "Don't leave yet. Can you stay for dinner? Mom made lasagna."

"I can't. I have some podcast business I need to take care of." Stacy walks me to the front door, and I give her a hug. "Thanks for listening."

"I'm not sure I was much help."

"You helped by sharing Jason's feelings about our mother. I owe it to him to give her a chance."

I drive home in a daze. I make myself a salad for dinner and sit down at my desk with a fresh legal pad. Texas has two senators—one in his first term and the other a thirty-six-year veteran currently on the long list of candidates for the next presidential election. Devin Pearson is considerably older than my mother, at least ten years her senior, with a head full of gray hair and beady dark eyes. I enlarge his photograph and study his features. Neither Jason nor I resemble our father.

According to Wikipedia, Pearson had no legitimate children, and his wife died ten years ago from cancer. When he's not in Washington, my biological father lives on his wife's family ranch about an hour outside of Austin.

I reach out to one of my contacts at the Austin Police Department. Albert Campbell is all too familiar with the senator's shady past. "He's as slippery as a snake," Albert says. "We have a long list of crimes we've been trying to pin on him. He keeps a team of first-rate lawyers on retainer and a gang of thugs on his payroll. Somehow, he gets reelected every six years. Why are you asking? Are you planning to interview him for your podcast?"

"I wish it were that simple," I say, and tell Albert about my relationship with the senator. When I discuss my plan with him, he agrees to help in any way.

I hang up with Albert and call my mother. She answers with a tipsy, "Hello." I hear loud noises in the background. Crowded bar noises. I imagine sitting beside her, sipping on a tequila. Will the alcohol craving ever go away?

"Did you, by any chance, bring documentation of my father's abuse with you?" I ask.

My question appears to sober her. "Yes. I have a file locked in the safe in my hotel room."

"Good. Bring them with you to dinner tomorrow night. I'll pick you up at six thirty. Where are you staying?"

"The Jefferson. I'll wait for you under the portico."

I end the call and stare down at the phone. *The Jefferson*? I've read none of Clara Thomas's books, but she must be excellent at writing love stories if she can afford the historic five-star hotel. Searching her long list of titles on Amazon, I download her most recent release—*To Love Again*—on my Kindle, hoping her protagonist will give me insight into my mother's character.

· · ·

I STAY UP LATE READING Clara Thomas's latest hit, and I sneak a few pages during my breaks at work the next day. I find the plot intriguing—the story of a middle-aged woman who finds love again after the tragic death of her husband. But the demure main character is different from the shameless protagonists I'm used to. And, instead of explicit sex scenes that leave me hot and bothered, the romance is limited to innocent kissing. Digging into product details on Amazon, I discover my mother's novels are considered sweet romance. This explains a lot.

As promised, my mother is waiting under the portico at the Jefferson Hotel looking like a runway model in a short suede skirt and a billowy sweater with bell-shaped sleeves. She's ditched the sunhat and pulled her golden hair back at the nape of her neck. I assume the documents I asked to see are inside the leather tote slung across her shoulder.

Climbing into the truck, she drops her bag on the floorboard and buckles her seat belt. "I didn't take you for a truck driver," she says, and we both laugh. She has Jason's sense of humor.

"The truck belonged to my late husband. But that's a story for another day," I say as I exit the Jefferson Hotel's parking lot back onto Main Street.

Her expression turns serious. "I'd like to hear about Lucas sometime."

I'm impressed. This woman has really done her homework.

She smooths out a wrinkle in her skirt. "I hope I'm dressed okay. I wasn't sure where we were going."

"You're fine. I made a reservation at Portico. It's about a twenty-minute drive out River Road."

She settles into her seat. "Oh good. I've been hoping for a tour of Richmond."

"You'll mostly see homes. Although many of those homes are impressive." I point out a few notable sites as we drive west on Main Street through the VCU campus.

Once we clear the business district, she settles into her seat. "So, do you know if the baby is a boy or girl?"

I shake my head. "I want to be surprised."

"Is the baby's father in the picture? In your podcast, you mentioned he was a friend."

I tighten my grip on the steering wheel. "No. He turned out to be a real jerk."

"Is there another special someone?"

Drew's image pops into my mind, bringing a smile to my face. "There was this one guy. We'd just started dating when . . ." My voice trails off. "Anyway, he blew me off when he found out about the baby."

I sense my mother studying me. "Have you explained the situation to him?"

"I've tried. He won't return my calls. I don't blame him. No guy in his right mind wants to raise another man's baby."

"You'd be surprised," she says in a you-never-know tone of voice.

"Ha. Maybe in one of your novels, but not in the real world."

"Dreams *do* come true in the real world, Jolie." Tilting her head to the side, my mother gives me a sassy smirk that reminds me so much of Jason it makes my heart hurt. In some ways, her comfortable companionship is much like my brother's. Chill bumps break out on my skin. I can't believe I'm talking to my mother in person. What if she doesn't go along with my plan? Will I be able to give her up?

"Not in mine," I say under my breath.

We arrive at the restaurant, and the hostess shows us to a table for two near the stone fireplace in the outdoor garden terrace. Our server arrives, and we order drinks and an appetizer to share. We make idle chitchat while we sip our beverages— pinot noir for her and decaf coffee for me. I confess I'm reading her newest release, which launches into a discussion about character development. My hostility toward her has waned. I have someone new to direct my anger toward. But our conversation remains guarded. We're still figuring each other out.

I wait until we're digging into our grilled artichokes and crab appetizer before asking, "Did you bring the documents with you?"

"In here." She pats the tote bag hanging from the back of her chair. "Would you like to look at them now? Or do you want to take them home with you?"

I glance around. It's too dark on the terrace for diners at nearby tables to see. But I want a chance to study them. "I'll look at them later."

She dabs at her mouth with her napkin. "You may find the photos difficult to stomach."

"I'm a cop. I'm sure I've seen worse." I'm convinced my plan is the only way. Although convincing my mother may take some doing. "This may be hard for you to understand, but I need closure. Over the years, I've experienced serious anger management issues as a result of being abandoned as a child. For most of my life, I've directed my anger at you. And now, I learn my father is responsible for breaking up our family. I've done my homework. Devin Pearson is a dangerous man who has gotten away with crimes more heinous than the ones he imposed on you. He needs to be stopped. And I intend to stop him."

My mother's face pales. "You don't know who you're dealing with, Jolie."

I hold her gaze. "I have a pretty good idea. He's eluded every branch of law enforcement."

"What makes you more equipped to bust him than the FBI?"

Her harsh tone stings. Then it sinks in. She's afraid for me. "At least hear me out," I say.

She nods and I tell her my plan. When I'm finished talking,

she says, "You're not looking for closure, Jolie. You want revenge."

I shrug. "Depends on how you look at it. I'm doing this. With or without your support."

She covers her mouth to hide her smile.

"Are you laughing at me?"

"Not at all," she says, lowering her hand to reveal a straight face. "You had a cat when you were little. Do you remember her? You named her Lucy."

"Are you sure? Because I hate cats. What does a cat named Lucy have to do with anything, anyway?"

"One day the cat climbed up in a tree and wouldn't come down. We had to call the fire department to get her out. You were quite taken with the female firefighter. She let you wear her helmet and sit behind the wheel of the hook and ladder truck. Just now, I had a flashback of your four-year-old self wearing that same determined expression and telling me, in no uncertain terms, you were going to be a firefighter when you grew up."

"Believe it or not, I considered being a firefighter for a while. But being killed by a bullet was more appealing than being killed by fire."

She drops her smile. "Are you always so blunt?"

"Jason was the nice guy. I'm the hard-ass. Funny thing, I understand my personality so much better now I know who my father is."

"You're nothing like your father, Jolie."

"Maybe. Maybe I'm just like him. We're about to find out. So, are you in, or aren't you?"

She falls back in her chair. "Truth be told, I'm tired of running. Even though Devin's goons haven't caught up with me in years, I am constantly looking over my shoulder, always on alert, never knowing when I might have to pack up and move. So, I'm in, but I have one condition."

I roll my eyes. "I'm afraid to ask."

"You take one of your police friends with you to Washington. You can't be alone when you confront your father."

A FINE LINE

I don't admit this to my mother, but in my case, when it comes to my father, there's a fine line between revenge and closure. I also had no intention of going alone to DC. Not in my condition. I need backup. And there's only one person I trust.

I text Calvin. *I need a favor that has nothing to do with the baby. Can you spare a few minutes today?*

Because today is Saturday, I expect him to be hanging out with Brenda. And I'm surprised when he responds immediately. *I'm at the station catching up on paperwork. I'll meet you at Starbucks in 30 mins.*

I give his text a thumbs-up and head out to my truck. I'm waiting in a booth with a cup of tea when he arrives. He grabs a coffee and joins me. "What's up?"

"My mother made a sudden reappearance in my life," I say, and tell him everything, including my idea to entrap my father.

"So, you're planning to bait him," Calvin says.

"Pretty much. I have to do this, Calvin. He's an evil man. Because of him, my mother has spent the last twenty-four years on the run. Because of him, Jason and I grew up in foster care. There's no telling how many other lives he's ruined."

"I get that you're angry, Jolie. You have every right to be. But you're pregnant. And what you're proposing is dangerous. *Extremely* dangerous. Why confront him? Why not turn everything over to the press and let them expose him?"

"Where's the fun in that? Are you going to help me or not?"

He points a finger at my belly. "Only because that baby you're carrying is mine," Calvin says with sparks shooting like daggers from his golden eyes.

"Great. I'll be in touch about the when and where," I say, sliding out of the booth.

"Wait! Where're you going? I need to know more about your plan."

"I'll tell you on the way to DC." I leave Calvin sitting in the booth alone. If he knows what I'm planning, he'll try to convince me to abort my mission. And I have no intention of doing that.

I spend the rest of the afternoon helping my mother move her things over from the Jefferson Hotel. She'll live with me until this situation with the senator plays out. For the first twenty-four hours, we tiptoe around each other, but we soon settle into a comfortable routine as roommates. The condo feels less lonely with her here, Jason's room less like a tomb.

I'd worried unnecessarily about having to entertain my mother. She works sixteen hours a day, writing and marketing her novels. During the free time she affords herself, she works out in our building's small fitness facility and makes elaborate meals for me. She's a fabulous cook, and I don't complain. We're not mother and daughter yet. Nor are we friends. But we're roommates, and that's a start.

If only I knew what to call her. My tongue gets hung up on the word *Mom*. She's Clara to her readers, and Sonya to those who knew her when. For now, I'll avoid calling her anything.

A phone call to the senator's DC office provides the information I need to proceed with my mission. The senator will be in Washington until Thursday of this week at which time he'll travel home to Austin for a long weekend. I text Calvin, alerting him to our departure time of four o'clock on Wednesday afternoon.

After work on Monday, I go to Home Depot and purchase a simple security system that will blast a loud siren and notify the police should an intruder break in through our front door. I spend the evening hours working on my podcast. I present the documented evidence my mother provides, and I interview her about the physical abuse she suffered at the hands of my father. My mother comes across as sincere in the video. That she's Clara Thomas, the mysterious romance author whom no one has ever seen, adds legitimacy to her story. I send a copy of the video to Albert Campbell in Austin with instructions for him to release it to the press in the event something happens to me.

When I call Albert, to put him on alert for potential trouble at the end of the week, he says, "I'm fully invested in taking this bastard down. I'll jump on a plane in a heartbeat if you need me."

"That means a lot. Hopefully, it won't come to that. But if it does, you're the first person I'll call."

I request the day off on Wednesday. I spend the morning going over and over the details of my plan until I've committed them to memory. My mother and I are seated at the kitchen island, eating a bowl of her homemade vegetable soup for lunch, when a wave of guilt overcomes me. She's spent years running from danger, and I'm willingly placing her in the line of fire.

"It's not too late to back out," I say. "If you leave now, you'll be halfway to Vermont by the time I arrive in Washington."

She vehemently shakes her head. "No way. I'm not going anywhere. I'll be right here waiting for you when you get back."

"Ugh. Now I know where I get my stubbornness."

She gives my shoulder a squeeze. "Damn straight. And don't you forget it."

"Do you know how to shoot a handgun? If so, Jason's is in a lockbox on the top shelf of his closet."

Sliding off her barstool, she retrieves her purse from the table by the door where she left it when she returned from the market earlier. She removes a holstered Sig Sauer pistol. "I bought this years ago. I'm actually a decent shot. You don't need to worry about me. I can take care of myself."

I unholster the gun, checking to make certain the barrel is empty, and hand it back to her. "Keep this with you at all times while I'm gone."

Around three o'clock, I dress in black—leggings, a boatneck tunic, and low-heeled booties. At three thirty, my mother walks me to the door.

She cups my cheek. "Please be careful, sweetheart. And just so you know, if something were to happen to me, I have encrypted backup files of all the documents on my computer and another set in a safe deposit box in Vermont."

"And you have Albert's contact information if something happens to me."

She tucks a stray strand of hair behind my ear. "Nothing's going to happen to either of us. I just got you back. I'm not letting you go again."

Calvin is waiting in front of the station when I swing by to pick him up. He tosses a bulletproof vest into the back and gets in the front beside me.

"Who's that for?" I ask, tossing my thumb over my shoulder at the vest.

He cuts his amber eyes at me. "You. Either you wear it, or I don't go."

"Fine. I'll put it on when we get to DC." I speed off through the streets of downtown to the interstate.

Neither of us speaks for the first twenty miles. Finally, Calvin breaks the silence. "Seriously, Jolie. I have a bad feeling about this. I did some digging. The senator is a really bad dude."

"Exactly. Believe it or not, he's on the long list of presidential candidates. We can't put an evil man like that in the White House."

I turn up the volume on the classic rock station, and for the rest of the way, I focus on the mission ahead of me.

As expected, the drive to DC at this time of day takes over three hours. I navigate the congested traffic to a luxury apartment building in Dupont Circle. I enter the parking garage and find an empty space on the ground level.

"Are you going to tell me the plan now?" Calvin asks.

"Just follow my lead." I open my car door and slide off the seat to my feet. Turning to face the truck, I tug my tunic over my head. I feel Calvin's eyes on my swollen belly as I adjust the bulletproof vest to fit my torso. I put my shirt back on, strap on a shoulder holster, and slide my arms into a long black puffer vest. I drop a switchblade and set of handcuffs in one pocket and a folded sheet of paper in the other. I buckle a black belt around me, which has handguns in holsters on each hip. "Let's do this thing," I say, and march off toward the elevator.

I punch a code into the keypad, and the elevator doors part.

Calvin's jaw drops. "How'd you manage that?"

"My cop friend in Austin has deep connections." On the ride up to the tenth floor, I say, "According to his agenda, Pearson should arrive home from an early business dinner in about thirty minutes."

Calvin picks the lock at number 136, and we scout out the

apartment, which is handsomely furnished with priceless antiques. But there are few personal touches. No family photographs. Only a handful of suits hang in the closet. No food in the refrigerator aside from a chunk of moldy cheddar cheese.

I'm seated in the dark on the couch, and Calvin is hiding in the coat closet in the small foyer when the senator arrives home. He flips on the light and starts toward the bedroom hall. He doesn't see me, and when I say, "Evening, Senator," he jumps back, his hand pressed to his chest.

He quickly composes himself. "Who are you, and why are you in my apartment?"

I stand and cross the room to him. Despite his age, he's even more handsome in person. He's elegantly dressed in gray flannel slacks and a tailor-made navy sport coat. He carries an air of power and wealth about him that makes him a formidable figure. "Look closely. Are you sure you don't know who I am?"

I watch for his reaction. Aside from a pulsing vein in his temple, he doesn't flinch. "Jolene Hogan. My darling daughter, we meet at last. It took you long enough to locate me." Pearson makes a *tsk tsk* sound with his tongue. "And you call yourself an investigator."

"You are an egomaniac, aren't you? Truth is, I haven't been looking for you. In fact, I didn't know you existed until a few days ago. My mother is the one I yearned for all those years I spent in foster care. I've never thought much about my biological father. I certainly have no memories of you. Good thing too. Memories of a father beating one's mother can cause irreparable psychological damage to a child. Coincidentally, I've seen documented proof of that abuse. I don't imagine your constituents would approve of how you treated your mistress. Even if it happened over two decades ago."

Pearson's jaw tightens, and he slips his hand in his pocket.

"What're you doing?" My gaze shifts slightly to the right, and over his shoulder, I see Calvin emerge from the coat closet.

"I'm calling my assistant," Pearson says, looking down at his phone as he taps on the screen. "To let him know he forgot to take out the trash."

Sneaking up on him from behind, Calvin wraps an arm around the senator's neck and presses the barrel of his handgun to his temple. "Drop the phone."

The senator's hands shoot up, and the phone falls to the Oriental rug with a thud.

"Who are you?" Pearson asks, squirming as he tries to get a glimpse of his captor.

Calvin tightens his grip on the senator. "I'm the father of Jolie's unborn baby."

I smooth my hand over my belly. "It's hard to tell I'm pregnant under this bulletproof vest. Congratulations, Senator! You're gonna be a granddaddy."

He pins me against the wall with his death stare. "What do you want?"

"Funny you should mention that." I remove the folded sheet of paper from my pocket. "Since I found out about you a few days ago, I've been doing a lot of research. What I learned disappointed me. You've been a very naughty senator. And I want you to confess your sins."

The color drains from Pearson's face.

"Don't worry. I have no intention of releasing your confession to the media." I raise my hand, finger pointed at the ceiling. "Except in the event something happens to my mother or me. In which case, your confession will immediately be released to the media. I believe they call it a dead man's switch. In my case, a dead woman's switch."

"I don't believe you."

I shrug. "That's your problem. Now . . ." I circle the room. "I think the lighting will be best with you seated on the sofa."

When I give Calvin the nod, he wrestles Pearson over to the sofa. I hand the senator the sheet of paper and step back with my phone's camera focused on him. "When I say *cheese*, you start reading."

Pearson looks down at the paper and back up at me. "I need my reading glasses."

"Of course. Where are they?"

"In the inside top pocket of my coat. May I?"

When Pearson moves his hand inside his blazer, Calvin pounces on him. Frisking him, Calvin removes a container of mace from his pocket along with the reading glasses. He tosses the reading glasses in the senator's lap and pockets the mace. "Try another stunt like that, Senator, and I will shoot you dead."

I click the Record button and say, "Cheese."

Pearson's hands shake as he reads the statement I've prepared outlining some of the worst crimes he's gotten away with over the years, including extortion and money laundering and treason.

When he's finished, I click the red button, ending the recording session. My phone makes a swish sound as I forward the video to Albert.

Eyes on my phone, Pearson says, "Who'd you send that to?"

"Someone I trust to keep it safe." I toss the handcuffs at Calvin. "Will you do the honor?"

Calvin forces Pearson onto his stomach and cuffs his hands behind his back. Placing Pearson's phone on the coffee table, I shatter the screen with the butt of my pistol. We turn out the lights as we exit the apartment. Silence fills the elevator on the way down. My adrenaline is pumping, but Calvin's tight expression lets me know he's pissed.

"You realize you just signed your own death warrant," he

says when we get in the truck. "Not only have you put your own life in danger but the lives of our unborn child and your mother as well."

"Your job is done, Calvin. Let me worry about our lives."

"You're a hard-ass, Jolene," he says, and I detect a note of admiration in his tone.

"Takes one to know one," I say, and start the engine.

"I saw the glint in your eye. You enjoyed torturing him. That's sick, Jolie. Make no bones about it. Pearson will come after you."

I put the truck in reverse. "And I'll be ready."

We leave the parking deck, and at the first stoplight, I thumb off a text to my mom. *Mission accomplished. We're on the way home.*

The traffic has thinned considerably, and we cruise through the downtown streets to the expressway. Replaying the encounter over and over in my mind, I'm elated by the outcome. Pearson was scared out of his mind. There's always a chance he won't retaliate. But I hope he does. I want nothing more than to make him pay for ruining my childhood, for making my mother live in fear all those years. Besides, the citizens of Texas deserve better from their elected officials.

Calvin and I don't speak again until Fredericksburg. "I'm starving," he says. "Can we stop for food?"

I realize I'm famished as well. I haven't eaten since lunch. "Sure. But we'll have to go through a drive-through. I want to get home to my mom."

I take the next highway exit and follow directions to Chick-fil-A. "Dinner's on me," I say as we pull up to the menu board.

"Ooh. Big spender," Calvin says and tells me his order.

Ten minutes later, we're cruising south on the interstate, stuffing waffle fries in our mouths, when Calvin declares, "I intend on being a part of this child's life."

"That's not necessary, Calvin. You're under no obligation."

"I don't feel obligated. I view raising a child an honor."

"Raising a child alone won't be easy. I need people I can count on. After the way you treated me, I doubt I'll ever be able to trust you again."

Calvin stops chewing, his bite of sandwich forming a lump in his cheek. "Seriously? I just saved your ass."

True. I couldn't have done it alone. "Okay, I'll give you five brownie points. You have ninety-five more to earn."

Calvin finishes chewing. "I tried to explain to you outside of the station that day, but you wouldn't listen. You and I have more in common than being hard-asses. We're kindred spirits. I've never experienced such a strong connection with anyone other than my sister. My feelings for you were scaring the hell out of me. And I ran."

"Right into Brenda's arms."

"Touché. I don't understand why women fall all over me."

I risk a glance at him. His expression is one of complete bewilderment. He totally doesn't get it. "Do you think it's because you encourage them?"

He shrugs. "Sometimes, maybe. But not always."

My eyes return to the road. "I'm in love with someone else, Calvin." I don't know what makes me say this. Perhaps the same fear Calvin experienced the night I kissed him.

"Oh, yeah? Who?" he asks, eyeing me suspiciously as he sucks on his straw.

"No one you know," I say, thinking of Drew. Is it true? Is it possible I'm in love with Drew? I was feeling something for him before . . . Could it have been love?

"How long have you been together?" Calvin asks, and I know what he's thinking.

I consider lying to him, but he saved my butt tonight, and I owe him the truth. "I started seeing him right before Jason died. But we've never slept together."

"What—"

I hold out my palm, shutting him up. "Give me a chance to explain before you interrogate me. I was messed up after Jason died. You saw me. You know. This guy, the one I'm in love with, tried to comfort me, and I turned him away. He hasn't spoken to me since he found out I'm pregnant."

Calvin's face lights up. "So, he's not in the picture. Which means I have a chance."

"Why would you want to be with me when I'm in love with another guy?"

"Because I don't believe you're in love with him." He drags his fingertips up my forearm, sending chills all over my body. "We could be really good together, Jolie."

I jerk my arm away. "I can't worry about this right now. Not until this Senator Pearson thing is over."

"That's fair," Calvin says. "Just don't shut me out again."

"Shut *you* out? You're the one who shut *me* out." I look over at him. There's a smirk on his lips. He's teasing me. "I've missed your friendship, Calvin. And I want my baby to know his father as long as said father can be a positive role model. But you and I can never be in a relationship. Even if you earn a thousand brownie points."

"We'll see about that," he says with that devilish smile I find hard to resist.

"I'm not kidding, Calvin. We're too much alike. We'd be butting heads all the time. We'd make each other miserable."

"Maybe. Or maybe we'd make each other blissfully happy. One thing's for sure, our lives would never be boring."

I remind myself to stay focused. Too many lives depend on it right now. "I'm going for an ultrasound on Friday. My mom is going with me, but you're welcome to come too."

"Seriously? I'll be there. Text me the details."

I wag my finger at him. "I'm warning you in advance. We're not finding out the sex. I want to be surprised."

He nods. "That's fine. I'd rather be surprised too."

I pull up alongside the curb outside the parking deck across from headquarters and shift in my seat toward him. "All joking aside, I'm grateful to you for helping me tonight."

"I'm not joking either when I say I'm worried about you, your mom, and the baby. You've unleashed the wrath of a very dangerous man. If anything happens, you call me anytime during the day or night." He kisses my cheek and gets out of the truck.

As I pull away from the curb, the feel of his lips lingers on my face, and his words ring out in my head. *Or maybe we'd make each other blissfully happy.* I'd hope we'd one day resume our friendship, but he's suggesting so much more. For the rest of the short ride home, I allow myself to consider the possibility of a serious romantic relationship between us. Calvin's ability to be faithful to only one woman is my primary concern.

My mother is waiting for me when I get home. We sit together on the sofa, and I walk her through the showdown with my father. "We have to be very careful these next few days, Mom. Whatever we do, we can't let our guards down."

She flashes a Cheshire Cat grin at me.

"Why are you smiling? I'm being serious. We're in danger."

"You just called me *Mom*."

My eyes widen. "I did? Is that okay?"

She puts an arm around me. "More than okay."

I tense at first, but when she pulls me in close, I relax against her body. I close my eyes and the years melt away. We're on the sofa in our rundown apartment in Austin. Jason is on her other side, and she's reading us a book. *Goodnight Moon.* We were four or five years old. I look up adoringly at her. She has a black eye.

No doubt from my father's hand. She never let us sense her fear. She kept us safe until she could no longer protect us. And then she gave us to someone who could.

She kisses my hair, and I snuggle in closer. At long last, we're mother and daughter again.

Near my ear, she says, "You had a visitor while you were gone."

I furrow my brow. "A visitor? Who?"

"A charming young man named Drew."

WATCH YOUR BACK

For the next two days, I'm constantly on alert, looking over my shoulder and around every corner. The enormity of the potential shitstorm I've brought to our doorstep hits home. I went after my father like a loose cannon, never stopping to consider the ramifications of my actions. I'm pregnant. I'm carrying a living being in my belly. Mom doesn't believe my father would harm his offspring, but I saw the look in the man's cold eyes. He'll take out anyone who threatens him, regardless of their DNA.

I see my fear reflected in my mother's eyes. But that fear is the elephant in the room we don't discuss. We both know what's at stake. We will protect one another at all costs. She doesn't leave the apartment while I'm at work. And I go to and from headquarters with no unnecessary stops.

The night after my trip to Washington, I wait until I'm alone in my room after dinner to call Drew. He answers right away, the cacophony of a crowded bar drowning out his voice.

"You're at work," I say.

"I am. But I can take a break. Hang on a second." I hear a

rustling noise and then the sound of a door closing. When Drew comes back on the phone, he asks, "So, how are you?"

"Fine. I'm sorry I missed you last night."

After an awkward moment of pleasantries, Drew says, "I'm sorry it's taken so long for me to come to my senses. I'm struggling to overcome my wounded pride. I can't stop thinking about what might have been. The baby could be ours."

"I was deranged with grief, and Calvin was there. He's a friend. His sister died in a car accident in college. He understood how devastated I was."

"Is he a friend with benefits?" Drew asks.

"On the worst day of my life, he was. And I took advantage of those benefits."

"Were the two of you ever involved romantically before that day?"

I think back months to the only other time Calvin and I slept together. I needed comforting that night as well. Lucas had died, and I'd learned of his affair with Nora Riley.

"No," I lie, because nothing good will come from Drew knowing the truth. For the baby's sake, I don't want things to be awkward between my baby daddy and my boyfriend. *If* my relationship with Drew even progresses that far.

Drew and I talk for a few more minutes. When he grills me about Calvin, I patiently answer his questions, even though I think most are none of his business. He tells me about work, and I explain about Mom's sudden reappearance in my life.

"I need to get back to work," Drew says finally. "But can we have dinner together soon? I owe you a home-cooked meal."

"I'd like that. But I have some personal stuff relating to my mom I need to work out first."

Drew lets out an irritated sigh. "Just call me when you're ready to get together," he says and hangs up.

I drop the phone on the bed beside me. The call leaves me with mixed emotions. Drew and I haven't seen each other in months. Is it possible our time apart has dimmed the spark we once shared? Or is a certain golden-eyed detective worming his way into my heart?

I tell Mom about the situation over oatmeal the following morning. "How can I have feelings for two men at once?"

"Happens all the time. My characters frequently find themselves in your predicament."

"And what advice do you give them?" I've grown accustomed to Mom talking about her characters as though they're actual people. In her mind, I guess they are.

"I encourage them to follow their hearts. Which isn't as easy as it sounds. Warning bells were sounding at an ear-splitting level when I first met your father. If only I'd learned earlier to trust my gut feelings, my life would've turned out differently." She places her hand over mine. "Then again, I wouldn't have you."

I give her a sad smile. I'm sorry her life has been so difficult because of me. I'm trying to make it better. But I'm worried my visit to see my father may have made it worse.

I think about warning bells while I finish my oatmeal. Bells clang loudly in my head whenever I'm with Calvin. Are they signaling a warning or summoning my attention?

As she does every morning, Mom walks me to the door and watches me go down the hall to the elevator. I call out to her before the doors close, "I'll pick you up a few minutes before eleven."

"I'll be ready," she yells back.

I'm not sure which of us is more excited about my ultrasound. Mom is convinced I'm having twins. Since I am one, the likelihood of me having fraternal twins is greater. But I secretly hope that's not the case. Having one baby is enough for me considering my complicated life.

Calvin is already in the waiting room when Mom and I arrive at the doctor's office. I marvel at the way the technician and nurses fall all over him. Even my mother flirts shamelessly with him. He's not overly friendly with them. In fact, sometimes he's borderline rude. But he's as excited as a boy at an NFL football game when he sees our fetus on the ultrasound machine.

The technician points out the baby's body parts as she runs the wand over my belly. "It's too early to tell the gender."

"Good!" Calvin says. "We don't want to know, anyway."

I like the way *we* sounds on his lips. Am I falling for this guy?

Calvin insists on taking us to lunch afterward. "My treat."

I shake my head. "No way! Being in a public place is too risky."

"Not if it's a crowded public place," he says, walking us to my truck in the parking lot.

"But I have to get back to work soon," I argue.

He says, "We'll go to Taste on Grove Avenue, where the service is quick."

I look at Mom, who shrugs. "Why not?"

During lunch, Calvin talks animatedly about the equipment the baby needs. "Some of these gadgets are supercool. I want to be there when you register."

I laugh out loud. "How do you know so much about baby stuff?"

"Google and Amazon."

Calvin has only taken a bite of his sandwich when he gets an urgent phone call. Wrapping up his sandwich, he says, "Sorry, ladies. I have to run. We got a break in a case I'm working on." He kisses my cheek and bolts for the door.

Watching him go, I ask Mom, "What do you think?"

"He's excited about the baby," Mom says, crunching on a chip.

My gaze shifts to Mom. "Duh. What do you think about Calvin as a person?"

"He's dark and mysterious, the type of man every woman dreams about having in her bed but not in her life."

"That's an interesting and accurate assessment." I remove the top slice of bread from my sandwich and peel off the unripe tomatoes. "What advice would you give your characters about a man like him?"

"To run fast and far," she says without hesitation.

"Do they listen to you?"

Mom laughs. "Rarely." She sets down her sandwich and wipes her lips. "Most women can't handle a man like Calvin. But you're strong and independent, Jolie. You can, if you so choose."

"He's such a man whore. I wonder if he has it in him to be faithful."

"You need to find out! Get to know him better. Dig deep. Learn what really makes him tick. In my limited experience as a romance writer, most men want the same thing—to find a woman they cherish, raise a family, and live the American dream."

Propping my elbow on the table, I plant my chin in my palm. "Drew is the one who comes to mind when I think of the American dream. How do you decide between two men?"

"You pick the one who lights your fire," Mom says. "And you don't choose until you're absolutely certain."

MOM and I spend a quiet weekend at home. We watch old movies and eat gallons of ice cream. Calvin comes over on Saturday afternoon to install a peephole in the door and ends up staying for dinner. We summon Grubhub to deliver our take-out order from Burger Bach. When the delivery guy arrives,

Calvin, with his eye pressed to the peephole, yells through the door for him to leave the order in the hall.

Despite being in imminent danger of my father's retaliation, Calvin is as relaxed as I've ever seen him. He teases my mom relentlessly, and to her credit, she gives it right back to him. She's sacrificed so much. She deserves a special someone in her life. Once this mess with the senator is out of the way, I aim to help her find him.

We eat at the kitchen island, lined up like The Three Stooges with me in the middle. Calvin says, "You should get a small table for dining."

"Where would I put it?" I ask, extending my arms toward the living room.

Calvin's eyes travel the room. "Good question. Things are pretty tight in here."

I get up and wander around the room. "Jason loved this open floor plan. I prefer rooms with specific purposes. One day I'm going to own a home with an eat-in kitchen. I'll position a pine farm table beside a picture window overlooking my fenced-in backyard where my children will play with our beagle named Sunshine, Sunny for short." I notice two sets of eyes staring at me, and I realize I've been thinking out loud.

"You've given your dream home a lot of thought," Calvin says.

Mom adds, "I so wanted to give you that dream home. My house in Vermont is the first property I ever owned. I bought it with you and Jason in mind. I'd always hoped the two of you would come live with me. Silly of me, I know. You were already grown and out on your own by then."

This brings a tear to my eye, and I hug Mom's neck from behind.

"Will you return to Vermont once the coast is clear?" Calvin asks Mom.

"If Jolie will still have me, I plan to move here. I'll rent some-where nearby so I can help with the baby while I'm getting to know the city better."

I rest my chin on Mom's shoulder. "Of course I'll have you. As a matter of fact, I just heard of a one-bedroom condo avail-able for rent on the fourth floor."

"That would be ideal, if you don't mind me being so close," Mom says.

"Mind? I'd love it." I press my face into her neck, inhaling her flowery perfume.

We share a private mother-daughter moment that would be awkward for most outsiders, but Calvin appears unfazed. He smiles at us as though he's happy for us. I'm happy for us too.

After dinner, we clean up and migrate to the living room to watch a movie. Calvin allows us to pick, and we choose a rom-com. I'm not surprised when, ten minutes in, he yawns.

He stands and stretches. "Ladies, I need to call it a night."

I get up to see him out. "Thanks for installing the peephole. And for staying for dinner."

"Thank you for having me." He dares to place a hand on my baby bump, and I don't brush it away. "When will you be able to feel the baby move?"

"Around eighteen weeks."

He pauses a beat to work out the date. "Which should be around the beginning of November."

"I'm impressed, Calvin. Most guys wouldn't know that."

"I'm not most guys, Jolie." He opens the door. "Lock this back, turn on the alarm, and don't let anyone in."

I salute him. "Yes, sir."

When I return to the sofa, Mom says, "Calvin is growing on me. That's not to say I didn't like him in the beginning. But I find it hard to trust someone so mysterious. He really seems to care about you and the baby."

"This isn't easy for him, but he's trying."

I pull the blanket over us and snuggle close to Mom. Jason is the only thing missing. And he's a big part of my world. But I'm grateful to have my mother back. She's like a drug. I can't get enough of her. I never want to be without her again.

We turn in after the movie. A FaceTime call from Drew wakes me from a deep sleep during the night. He's drunk. His words are slurred, and one eyelid is drooping. Sitting up in bed, I set the phone on a pillow in my lap, propped up against my knees.

"Are you just getting home from Carrigan's?" I ask.

"Yep. Some of us stayed after work to party. I was thinking about you earlier. I miss your visits to the bar."

"Gosh. That seems like a long time ago. So much has happened since then." My mind travels back to those lonely nights when my marriage was on the rocks and I desperately needed someone to talk to. I don't envision any trips to any bars in my future. And that's okay. I'm establishing a new life for myself with more constructive goals.

Drew closes one eyelid as he focuses on his phone's screen. "You look good, Jolie."

I snicker. "I look fat. But thank you, anyway."

"You're gonna get fatter before this is over."

My smile fades. "That's the wrong thing to say to a pregnant woman."

He appears to sober a little. "Right. Sorry. What'd you do tonight?"

"Mom and I ordered takeout and watched a movie."

"I don't get it, Jolie. How can you forgive your mom so easily after what she did to you?"

Irritation crawls across my skin. "I couldn't stay mad at her when I found out why she abandoned us. I've been so wrong about her all these years. I'm thrilled to have her back in my life. Have you ever considered finding your mom, Drew?"

"Hell no! I never want to see that bitch again."

My heart goes out to him. I felt like that about my mother not so long ago. "You might be surprised to learn why she took off. I certainly was."

"In my mind, there's never a good enough reason to abandon your child. What if *your* life goes south? Will you ditch your kid?"

I place my hand on my baby bump. No one can keep my child safer than me. I don't know how to respond, so I change the subject. "I went for an ultrasound yesterday. It's too early to tell the sex. But we got to see the baby. Everything appears normal."

Drew's expression contorts into an angry scowl. "Did your baby daddy go too?"

"Jealousy is not a good look, Drew. You've obviously been drinking. We should talk some other time." I click the red button, ending the chat.

Setting my phone on the nightstand, I slip beneath the covers. But I don't fall back asleep for hours. I don't like what I just saw in Drew. Is it possible I was wrong about him? Then again, I should give him a break. I've made plenty of drunk calls I later regret.

Sure enough. When I wake around ten on Sunday morning, I have a long string of texts from Drew, apologizing for his behavior. I send a brief reply. *No worries. We're good.* Although something warns me we're not good. We're not on the same page. Or even in the same universe.

Mom and I spend the rest of the morning in the workout room, and after lunch, we order a week's supply of groceries from a delivery service. I keep her company, perched on a barstool and sipping hot tea, while she makes homemade marinara sauce.

"How did you and the senator meet?" I ask.

She looks up at me from dicing tomatoes. "I worked in his Austin office. I was one of his speechwriters."

"No kidding! So you've always been a writer?"

Her gaze shifts back to the tomatoes. "I majored in English in college. But writing speeches is way different from writing romances."

"Where'd you go to college?" I ask, realizing there's so much I don't know about her.

"TCU," she says, more to the cutting board than to me.

My mouth falls open. TCU is one of the most expensive in Texas. I know this from when Jason was applying to colleges. I think back to my conversation with Drew last night. Perhaps I *was* too quick to forgive my mom.

Sliding off the barstool, I move around to the other side of the island, closer to her. "I assumed, because you left us in the foster system, you had no other family who could help take care of us. Do you have siblings? What about your parents? I assumed they were poor. But not too poor if they could afford to send you to TCU."

Mom sets down her knife and turns to face me. "I'm the only child of extremely religious Southern Baptist parents. My father earned a modest living as an appliance repairman. I worked hard in school and was rewarded with a full ride scholarship."

"So that's where Jason got his brains."

Her lips part in a sad smile. "My parents disapproved of my relationship with the senator. And rightly so. He was a married man. The bruises were still fresh from my last beating when I paid them a visit. I asked them to keep you and Jason until I could get my life together. They refused, told me I'd made my bed and I would have to lie in it. I never spoke to them again after that. They're both dead now." Her eyes are wet with tears when she turns back around and begins shredding fresh basil.

While I'm dying to know more, now is not the right time to ask.

When dinner is ready, Mom pops the cork on an expensive bottle of red, pouring a splash into a glass for me, and we sit down to eat at the island.

Ignoring her dinner, Mom sits back on the barstool, crossing her legs as she sips her wine. "Your father and I were very much in love in the beginning. As his speechwriter, I traveled with him to many of his speaking engagements. His marriage was on the rocks. He desperately wanted children, but his wife claimed she couldn't conceive. I think she was faking. She hated to ruin her perfect figure or interrupt her social life.

"I tried to trick him into marrying me by getting pregnant. I *accidentally*"—she uses air quotes—"forgot to use my diaphragm one night. Once he got over his anger, we were actually okay for a couple of years. Believe it or not, he doted on you and Jason. He loved you kid, as much as a heartless man like Devin could love anyone. But then I began putting pressure on him to leave his wife. It backfired. And that's when he began abusing me."

I see the anguish in her face. Confessing her sins is difficult for her. "Thank you for telling me. I appreciate your honesty."

She sets down her wineglass and lifts her fork. "We have much to learn about each other. It'll all come out in time."

There's nothing I can do about the time we've lost. But there's plenty I can do about the future. I won't doubt this woman again.

ON MONDAY MORNING, Mom walks me to the door when I leave for work. As the elevator doors close, I yell at her to have a good day.

I've been watching and waiting for four days now. I expected my father's goons to strike over the weekend, not first thing on a Monday morning. I'm off my game and fail to notice the dark figure hiding in the back seat of my truck. I'm buckling my seat belt when a hand clamps over my mouth from behind.

"Scream, and I'll shoot you dead," a deep voice whispers loudly in my ear. The barrel of his gun is cold and hard against my temple.

He snatches my bag from the passenger seat. My phone and gun are both inside. He presses an object against my ear, and I hear my mother's voice. "Do as they say, Jolie."

I've put several safety measures in place in the event something like this happens. I pray they go into effect.

My eyes dart right and left and up at the rearview mirror. Even though it's rush hour, none of the building's other tenants are in sight. He drags me out of the truck and over to the service elevator. He's done his homework. The elevator is out of the way and hardly ever used. We ride up to my floor, and he walks me to my condo.

Mom is seated on the sofa with her hands bound behind her. Gray duct tape is wrapped around her ankles with another strip covering her mouth. Her blue eyes are wide with fear. Behind her stands a man dressed in black with a black stocking cap covering his head and face.

My captor pushes me hard, and I land on the sofa beside her. "Don't worry," I whisper. "Help will be here soon."

"Shut up, bitch!" My captor, who's dressed identically to his partner, comes at me with a roll of duct tape.

He holds my phone near my hands. "Enter your password."

I tap in the password. I've warned both Albert and Calvin to be aware of strange texts from me. "If I have important information to share, I will call you with it," I told them. "If you get a request from me via text, someone most likely has gotten hold of my phone."

The other man opens my laptop. I've booby-trapped it as well. I created a new default user under the name Jolene Hogan instead of Jolie Hogan, and I've spent an inordinate amount of time making this user account look like the real deal. With the help of a computer genius in the department, I've programmed my account to email Calvin and Albert in the event someone accesses this account.

I squeeze my eyes shut and say a silent prayer that everything goes according to my intricate plan. I need to buy us some time. I kick and scream and thrash about on the sofa, which earns me a fist to the right side of my face. The room spins, and I crumple against my mom. The men hover over my computer, talking in a language I don't recognize or understand. My mind races as I consider distraction tactics. I'm limited with my hands and ankles bound. I don't want to jeopardize my baby's life, but if I don't do something, we're all dead.

The men slam the computer shut and come after us, hoisting Mom and me off the sofa and dragging us down the hall to Jason's bedroom. They rake Mom's shoes and other belongings from the closet floor and then toss us inside like bags of garbage. One man produces a device from a black leather tote bag. I saw similar fake devices when I was at the police academy. He punches a button, and the timer on the bomb begins to tick. Thirty minutes and counting. My wide eyes find Mom's. We are so screwed.

BOOM

The timer glows red in the pitch-dark closet, counting down our last minutes to live. I can't see Mom, but I hear her sniffling and feel her body trembling beside me. This is all my fault. I put my mom's life in danger. And if I don't do something, my baby will never be born.

My mind races as I think of a plan. It's a stretch, but the only option I have. I stand up slowly, which isn't easy with my feet bound. I bang my head against the coat hangers until one falls to the floor. Dropping back to my bottom, I feel around on the floor with my bound hands until I locate it. The hanger is the wire kind from the dry cleaners. Untwisting the wires at the neck, I cut at the duct tape with the semisharp end.

The process is excruciatingly slow. I drop the hanger multiple times. Sweat breaks out on my forehead and trickles into my eyes, stinging them. I blink hard. When the timer reaches the ten-minute mark, I've torn enough of the tape to wrench my hands free. Ripping the tape from my mouth and ankles, I throw open the door. Darting across the room to the nightstand, I retrieve the pocketknife Jason kept in the top drawer and cut the tape from Mom's ankles. I don't bother with her hands. There isn't time. We have eight minutes to get out of the building.

We're racing down the hallway toward the living room when Calvin explodes through the door.

I shout at him. "There's a bomb! We have to get out now!"

He motions us to the door. "Go! Take the stairs."

I stare at him. "Aren't you coming?"

"Not yet. I've had some training. I'll try to diffuse it. Where's the bomb?"

"In Jason's closet, first room on the left." Mom and I sprint down the hall to the stairwell and run down ten flights of stairs.

The lobby is empty, and through the glass entrance doors, I see Calvin's unmarked car, the only vehicle parked on the curb. Did he not radio for backup? With no phone to call for help, I smash the glass on the fire alarm panel with my elbow and pull the lever, summoning the fire department.

We exit the lobby. There's little traffic on the street. Flagging down a passing car, I instruct the startled woman to call 9-1-1. "There's a bomb in that building," I say and give her the address.

Shielding our eyes from the bright sun, we stare up at the building, watching and waiting for the explosion. Nothing happens. More than eight minutes have passed. Was Calvin able to defuse the bomb?

First responders surround the building, and uniformed officers cordon off the block. Mel and Captain Winnie arrive together. I quickly explain about the bomb. "Calvin's inside! He's trying to defuse it."

As the words leave my mouth, Calvin exits the building. "It was a simple device. The damage to the building would've been minimal." He looks back and forth between Mom and me. "But that closet would've blown to smithereens with the two of you in it."

The captain lifts her radio to her ear and barks, "Send in the bomb squad."

When the squad arrives minutes later, Calvin ushers them upstairs to the condo while I explain the situation to the captain.

In a scolding tone, the captain says, "You purposefully baited your father, putting many lives in danger. Including your unborn child's."

I hang my head. "I'm aware. But he's an evil man. He's ruined many lives, including my mother's. He cost me my childhood."

Winnie draws me in for a half hug. "You're alive," she whispers. "That's all that matters."

Thirty minutes pass before Calvin returns with the bomb squad, announcing the condo secure. "But Jolie and her mom are not out of danger yet. I'm assigning myself to this case," he says to Winnie, his features etched in stone as though daring her to challenge him.

Two clean-cut men dressed in suits and wearing dark sunglasses approach. They simultaneously flash badges. "FBI. We're looking for Jolene Hogan." One is in his thirties, a ginger with freckles dotting his face, and the other older with dark hair graying at his temples.

I tentatively raise my hand. "I'm Jolene."

The older agent glances around. "Is there somewhere we can talk?"

Calvin extends a hand to them. "Calvin Ingram, detective in charge of this case. Let's go upstairs to Jolene's condo." He dismisses the captain with a curt I've-got-this nod of his head.

Mom and I follow the law enforcement officers into the lobby and file into the elevator behind them. We introduce ourselves on the way up to the tenth floor. The ginger is Agent Cook, and the other man, Agent Soto.

When we reach the condo, Mom excuses herself to make

coffee while Calvin settles me on the sofa. "Are you okay? You had quite a scare."

"I'm fine," I say, even though my near-death experience has shaken me to the core. Dodging bullets is one thing. Watching the timer run out on one's life is another matter entirely.

I look from Cook to Soto. "I assume you're here about my father, Senator Pearson. Who sent you?"

"We saw your video," Cook says.

Calvin rests a hand on my shoulder. "When Campbell received your email this morning, as instructed, he released your video to the world."

"You've made some pretty serious allegations against the senator," Soto says.

Anger propels me off the sofa. "Allegations of extortion, money laundering, and treason. The FBI is well aware of my father's crimes. You've had evidence against him for decades, but you've yet to bring charges against him. Why is that, Agent Soto?"

"Because the evidence isn't strong enough," Soto says.

"You're lying. I've seen the evidence."

"You need to stay out of the way, Ms. Hogan, and let us do our jobs. You damn near got yourself killed today." Soto's gaze shifts from me to Calvin. "We're taking over the case."

Calvin jumps to his feet. "Like hell you are. This is my territory. This bombing incident happened in my city. Our officers are already working the case. We're searching the building for the suspects, and we're pulling surveillance video from security cameras. We won't rest until Senator Pearson is behind bars. You can either cooperate with us, or you can get out." He aims his thumb over his shoulder at the door.

Soto sighs loudly. "Okay. But we need to know everything. So, leave nothing out."

Mom arrives with a tray loaded with mugs of coffee and the

fixings. Setting the tray on the coffee table, she sits down beside me. Mom and I take turns talking, telling them everything, beginning with Mom's affair with Pearson. When I tell them about my recent trip to DC, their expressions remain tight, but they don't chastise me. Maybe they sense my distress. I'm over-whelmed with exhaustion and a sense of dread that weighs heavily on me.

Within the hour, the condo is teeming with FBI agents and police officers. Mom and I retreat to our rooms, but I leave my door ajar, so I can listen out for important developments.

I'm lost without my electronic devices. The bombers took my cell phone and computer, and my iPad is dead. I plug it in to charge and crawl in bed beneath the covers. I close my eyes, but I'm too on edge to sleep. From the voices in the other room, I learn the security footage revealed a snippet of a license plate believed to belong to the bombers. FBI agents in DC have been dispatched to arrest my father. My video has gone viral. Even the twenty-four-hour news channels are picking it up. And an officer found my electronic devices in a trash can in the parking garage. Calvin has sent the devices to headquarters for fingerprinting, which is unnecessary since both bombers were wearing gloves. I want to tell Calvin not to bother, but I lack the energy to get out of bed.

Calvin comes in to check on me around three in the after-noon. "You don't look well, Jolie. You need to eat. What can I fix for you?"

The thought of food makes me feel nauseous. "I'll get some-thing in a while. Have there been any developments?"

"Well, let's see." He eases down to the side of the bed, but he doesn't tell me anything I don't already know. He pulls the covers tight under my chin. "You're safe now, Jolie. I won't let anyone get to you."

"Do you think Captain Winnie will fire me?"

He shakes his head. "I spoke to her a little while ago. She's terribly worried about you, but she's not upset. You may get a lecture at some point, but I can't see her disciplining you."

"Good." I close my eyes, pretending to be asleep, but when he leaves the room, I unplug my iPad from the charger. My video is the top post on all the important social media platforms, and all the major news sources report a nationwide manhunt underway for Senator Devin Pearson. I have several texts from Drew, who has heard about the bomb and seen my video. I respond, letting him know I'm okay. He wants to talk, but I tell him I don't have my phone.

Late afternoon, the din of voices in the other room diminishes to silence. I venture out of my room around six o'clock. Mom is alone in the kitchen making tea. "Where is everyone?" I ask.

"I'm not sure. I've been writing all afternoon." She hands me the tea and puts another cup on to brew. "Did you get some sleep?"

"No, I'm too keyed up." I burst into tears. "I'm so sorry, Mom. I never meant for things to go this far."

She takes me in her arms. "Of course, you didn't. Nothing good will come from obsessing about what might have been. Thanks to you, we are safe."

"You mean, thanks to Calvin."

She holds me at arm's length. "Calvin saved the building. *You* saved us. I admire your courage, sweetheart. If not for you, I would've spent the rest of my life living in fear. With any luck, the authorities will find your father and throw him in prison for the rest of his life."

I nod, biting down on my quivering lower lip. Something tells me it won't be that easy.

My heart skips a beat when the front door swings open. I reach for my gun, but it's not there. The bombers took it. Calvin appears in the doorway, and I slump against the counter. "Geez, Calvin, you scared the hell out of me."

"Sorry." He holds up two take-and-bake pizzas from Superstars Pizza. "I brought dinner."

"Thanks," I say, even though the thought of food turns my stomach. "Did anyone find my weapon?"

"Not yet." He sets the pizzas down on the counter and preheats the oven. "Are you ladies hungry?"

"You two eat without me." I brush past him on my way to Jason's room. I'm relieved to find Jason's gun safe is still on the top shelf of his closet. I punch in the code and remove the gun. Inserting the loaded magazine, I stuff the gun into my waistband and return to the living room.

Calvin insists on making a plate of food for me. I sit with them at the island, but my stomach is too knotted up to eat. Mom eyes my untouched food. "You need to eat, sweetheart. To keep up your strength for the baby."

I push the plate away. "I'm sorry. I don't feel well."

"You look a little pale." Mom presses the back of her hand to my forehead, as though I'm a child and she's checking for fever.

I brush her hand away. "I'll be fine."

Calvin's phone vibrates on the counter with a call from Agent Soto. He takes his phone over to the window, out of earshot. Minutes later, he returns to the island and says, "The FBI apprehended the bombers. They were on the way back to DC. The bombers are singing like canaries. According to them, the senator employs an army of thugs to do his dirty work."

My heart sinks. "I was afraid of that. The senator's reach is broad. We may never be free of him. Any update on his location?"

Lifting a slice of pizza, Calvin says, "Not yet. The bombers claim to know nothing of his whereabouts."

"Of course they do." Standing up, I take my plate around the island, drop the pizza slices into a plastic storage bag, and scrape the Caesar salad down the disposal. "I need to lie down. I'll be in my room if you hear anything."

I'm stretched out on my bed, surfing social media websites on my iPad, when my mother taps on the door a few minutes later. "Come in," I say.

She enters the room and sits down on the edge of the mattress. "Calvin and I are worried about you, sweetheart. You're under a lot of stress, which isn't good for the baby. And today was . . . traumatic. If you're not feeling well, we should call your doctor."

"Stop worrying. I told you, I'm fine." Mom winces at the sound of my irritated tone. I didn't mean to lash out at her. What is wrong with me? "I'm sorry. I'm not myself right now."

Mom nudges me over and lies down beside me. "We love you, honey. Of course we're going to worry about you and the baby."

I let out a grunt. "Calvin loves the baby. Not me." Now I sound like a love-struck teenager. This day needs to end.

Mom fingers a lock of hair out of my face. "You're wrong about that. Your detective is quite smitten with you."

I roll over onto my side, putting my back to her. "No, he's not. He's smitten with the idea of us being a family. He's hung up on doing the honorable thing."

"Being a family isn't a bad thing, Jolie."

"Trust me. I know how Calvin Ingram operates. First pretty girl that comes along, and he'll revert to his old ways."

Mom spoons me from behind. "I think you're wrong about him. Why don't you give him a chance? Or do you have your heart set on Drew?"

"Right now, I have my heart set on sending the senator to prison. I can't think of anything else."

"I'm sorry, Jolie. I'm being insensitive. I was trying to distract you, to make you think about something other than your father. I guess that's impossible."

I roll back over to face her. "We nearly died today. But you seem so calm and collected. I don't get it. Why aren't you upset?"

"Because we *didn't* die today." She runs a finger down my cheek. "And even if we had, I would've died a happy woman because I found you. And because I know Jason is waiting for us in heaven."

I remember feeling like this not so long ago. When I first went back on patrol, I acted recklessly, hoping I'd die so I could be with Jason. I rub my belly. But I'm pregnant now. And I want to give my child a chance at life as well as all the things I never had.

Mom sits up. "Let's call your doctor, to see if she can give you something to relax."

"No! Drugs aren't good for the baby. I just need some sleep. I'll feel better tomorrow."

Mom kisses her fingertips and presses them against my forehead. "Promise to call me if you need me?"

I kiss the tip of my pointer finger and touch her lips. "I promise."

Mom leaves and Calvin soon comes into the room. "Your mom says you're turning in. If it's okay with you, I'm going to stay here tonight. On the sofa."

I bolt upright. "You don't have to do that, Calvin. We have officers stationed outside the door to protect us. Go home and get some sleep. Or go see Brenda." I throw this jab in to see how he reacts.

"I broke up with Brenda."

"Really? Who's the new girl?"

"A certain smoking-hot cop who's carrying my baby." Placing his hands on my shoulders, he pushes me back down in bed. "Now, get some rest."

"There are extra pillows and a blanket at the top of my closet." I should get out of bed and help him, but my body feels too heavy.

He removes an armful of linens from the closet. "I'll be right outside if you need me."

I smile at him. "Thanks, Calvin. For everything."

He winks at me. "You bet." He turns out the light and pulls the door to, leaving a crack in case I need to call him.

Calvin has changed since our trip to Washington. Or has he? Is this his true self? The real Calvin Ingram who nurtured me the weeks after Jason died.

Closing my eyes, I fall asleep thinking about what the real Calvin will be like as a father.

Shortly before midnight, I wake with abdomen cramps. My first thought is, I've started my period. Then I remember I'm pregnant. I get out of bed and plod on bare feet into the bathroom. When I pull my pajama bottoms down to use the potty, the sight of blood on my underwear shocks me, and I let out a little scream.

Calvin and Mom appear in the doorway. I look up at them from the toilet. "I'm bleeding. I think I'm having a miscarriage."

Mom and Calvin exchange a look. "I'll get our things," Mom says, backing out of the bathroom.

"Come on. Let's get you to the hospital," Calvin says, helping me up from the toilet.

Meeting us in the hallway, Mom hands me my purse and a fleece to slip on over my pajamas.

The officers stationed outside our door are surprised to see us emerge from the condo. "Is something wrong," the younger of the two asks.

"We have a medical emergency," Calvin explains. "You two stay here. Don't let anyone in."

In the parking garage, Calvin helps me into the back seat of his unmarked sedan. "Which hospital?"

"Henrico Doctors'," I say.

With blue lights flashing, we speed through the empty downtown streets to the expressway. Mom uses Calvin's phone to call my doctor's after-hours number. When she ends the call, Mom reports, "Good news! Your doctor is on call. The operator is notifying Dr. Reid to let her know we're on the way."

I pull my fleece over my face to stifle the sound of my crying. This baby means the world to me. I can't bear the thought of losing it. This is all my fault. If only I'd been more careful.

Fifteen minutes later, we pull into the emergency room parking lot. A striking nurse with milk chocolate skin instructs Mom and Calvin to stay in the waiting room until I get settled.

"My name is Kendra," the nurse says on the way to the examining room. "Dr. Reid is expecting you. She's delivering a baby at the moment, but she'll be with you soon."

Helping me change into a hospital gown, Kendra checks my vitals and quizzes me about the symptoms I've been experiencing. She leaves me alone to stare at the clock. Thirty minutes pass before Dr. Reid finally arrives around one o'clock.

"Sorry, I got tied up with a delivery."

I study her as she consults my chart. She's a serious woman with curly mahogany hair pulled back in a messy bun at the nape of her neck.

She comes to stand beside the bed. "I saw the headline news. You're lucky to be alive, Jolie. I thought you were working a desk job until the baby arrives."

"I am. But this case is personal. The senator is my biological father."

The doctor lets out a little gasp. "I'm so sorry."

"Can stress cause a miscarriage?" I ask.

"There's no evidence of that. Although excessive stress like you experienced today certainly isn't good for the baby."

I choked back a sob. So, I killed my baby.

Dr. Reid performs a pelvic exam and declares my cervix hasn't dilated. When she runs the wand of the fetal Doppler across my belly, at the sound of my baby's heartbeat, I let out a breath I didn't know I was holding.

The doctor gives my shoulder a reassuring squeeze. "These are both good signs. Let's get some blood work. Is anyone here with you?"

I nod. "My mom and the baby's father are in the waiting room."

"I'll tell Kendra to call them back," the doctor says and exits the room.

Five minutes later, Kendra returns with Mom and Calvin in tow. The nurse draws three vials of blood and disappears again.

"Has there been any word about the senator?" I ask Calvin.

"Not yet." He wags a finger at me. "But you need to stop worrying about the senator and think about the baby."

"I'm trying. It's not that easy. Besides, we heard the baby's heartbeat. I think everything is fine."

The doctor returns. After I make the introductions, Calvin hits her with a lot of questions, which she answers patiently and knowledgeably. "When we get the results from the blood test, if everything appears normal, I'll send her home on bed rest."

"For how long?" I ask, alarmed.

"A few days," Dr. Reid says. Maybe a week. Until the bleeding stops, and we know for certain you're out of the woods."

My gaze shifts to Calvin, who has moved over near the door and is talking on his phone. His voice is hushed, and his brow pinched. Normally, I wouldn't be concerned, but it's almost two thirty in the morning. I wait until he hangs up before asking, "Who was that? What's going on?"

He casts a nervous glance at the doctor. "Your friend Albert in Austin. The FBI apprehended the senator. He was trying to cross the border into Mexico. It's over, Jolie. Your father is in prison and you're out of danger."

"I need to be certain. Give me that phone! I want to talk to Albert." I yank the covers back and swing my legs over the side of the bed. A piercing pain stabs me in the belly, stealing my breath. I double over, letting out a loud groan.

"That's it!" The doctor gestures at the door. "Everybody out of the room. Stat."

MAGIC WORDS

The medicine dripping from an IV bag puts me in a lala haze. When I fully regain consciousness thirty-six hours later, I'm in a private hospital room. Vases of flowers line the windowsill, and a bouquet of balloons is tied to the arm of a lounge chair. Mom and Stacy are standing at the foot of the bed, whispering. I hear other voices too, Calvin's and Dr. Reid's, coming from outside the open door in the hallway.

My hand finds my belly, and I'm relieved to feel the bump that is my baby. I clear my throat. "Is the baby okay?"

Stacy and Mom move closer to the head of the bed. Mom leans over and kisses my cheek. "Welcome back, sweetheart."

Stacy strokes my arm. "Your baby is fine."

My eyes flutter shut. "Thank God," I say with a sigh. "What happened?"

"Your blood pressure shot dangerously high. Given the circumstances, Debra . . . Dr. Reid decided it best to sedate you."

I open my eyes wide. "Won't the meds harm the baby?"

"Not the ones she used."

Dr. Reid and Calvin enter the room and approach the side of the bed opposite Mom and Stacy. An eerie feeling overcomes me. I feel as though I'm on my deathbed, surrounded by my loved ones. I want out of this bed and this hospital.

I lock eyes with the doctor. "Stacy says the baby is fine. Can I go home?"

The doctor holds up a finger. "On one condition. Stacy stays with you."

"But Stacy has to work," I argue.

Stacy shakes her head. "Not at the moment. I'm in between jobs. I don't start with my new practice for another two weeks."

"Fine." I look over at Calvin. His expression is grim and he's unusually quiet. "What aren't you telling me?"

Calvin glances at the doctor who nods her head. "We have some news. Dr. Reid is worried how it will affect you."

Dr. Reid says, "I want you to hear it now, while you're still in my care."

My eyes dart about, landing on each of them in turn. "What is it, already?"

"The senator is dead," Calvin blurts. "He was strangled to death in prison. Apparently, he had a lot of enemies."

The song "Ding Dong! The Witch is Dead" comes to mind. "I won't have a meltdown, if that's what you're worried about," I say to my doctor. "The senator hurt a lot of people. He deserved what he got. Now, when can I go home?"

The doctor laughs. "As soon as I sign the release papers. Today is Wednesday. I want you to finish out the work week on bed rest. *If* you have no more bleeding, you can resume your normal life this weekend." She opens her iPad and makes a note of the reading on the blood pressure monitor behind my head. "Stress affects people in different ways, Jolie. You were lucky this time. Don't push the envelope."

~

MOM AND CALVIN insist on pampering me. Since there's nothing I can do about it, I let them fuss. Stacy and Mom become fast friends. They talk in the living room for hours, which keeps them off my back so I can focus on my podcasts. Calvin returns my electronic devices, and I spend an afternoon going through emails, texts, and voice messages. My social media followers request more information about the senator, and I plot my next podcast to include a lengthy interview with Albert Campbell. He played a major role in breaking the case, and he deserves some of the glory. My nationwide law enforcement network continues to grow, along with my list of potential interviewees.

I'm surprised, and oddly relieved, when I don't hear from Drew. On Monday morning, Dr. Reid clears me to return to work. When I leave headquarters on Tuesday afternoon, I drive over to Carrigan's. Through the window, I spot Drew flirting with a pretty blonde customer. I was once in this customer's seat. I recognize the twinkle in his blue eyes. He's love struck. And I'm happy for him. We had chemistry. But we grew apart before we ever had a chance to come together.

Mom signs a year lease on the one-bedroom apartment on the floor below me. At the end of October, when she returns to Vermont to organize her move, Calvin insists on staying with me. He's scarcely let me out of his sight since my near miscarriage. He won't admit it, but I can tell he's worried about the potential for additional fallout from the senator's case. I don't argue. I'm enjoying his company more and more.

After work on Friday night of the first week in November, he takes me out for an early dinner at Shagbark, an upscale American food restaurant located in Libbie Mill Midtown. We're seated at a window table for two, sharing an appetizer of pan-roasted mussels, when Calvin says, "What say we get married? You're having my baby. We should be a family."

His proposal doesn't surprise me. I've sensed it coming for

some time. He wants to get married for some of the right reasons. Just not for all the right reasons. He failed to mention his feelings for me. Or lack thereof. His shady past is hard to ignore. Then again, I have my share of skeletons in the closet. My fondness for him continues to grow. If I let myself, I could easily fall head over heels in love with him. But I already have one failed marriage under my belt. And only a few months ago, I thought I was in love with Drew. I need to be certain of my feelings for Calvin.

"I'm not ready for a commitment, Calvin. After everything that's happened this year, I need time for myself. And time to spend with my mom. We're just getting to know each other again."

He appears wounded. "You don't trust me."

I stare down at my plate. "That's part of it. You have quite the reputation. There are few women in the department you haven't slept with. I'm not a fan of open marriages. Our friendship is solid. At least we're getting there. We can raise this baby together, as mother and father, without getting married."

"Despite what you might think of me, I'm not a fan of open marriages either. I—"

The waiter interrupts him when he arrives with our entrees —maple-brined pork chop for him and grilled salmon for me.

"What were you about to say?" I ask, once the waiter has gone.

"I'm turning over a new leaf. I haven't slept with anyone since Brenda. And believe me, many women have tried."

"See!" I stab my finger at him. "Those many women are what I'm talking about. You're staying away from those women now, because you think you're ready to get married and have a family. What happens after we've been married a few years and you grow tired of me? What's going to stop you from sleeping with them then?"

He cuts a bite of pork chop and stuffs it into his mouth. "I can't believe I'm admitting this to you, but sleeping around always made me feel dirty." He shakes his head, as though disgusted with himself. "Listen to me. I sound like a woman. But it's true. I was looking for fulfillment. Instead, every sexual encounter I had with a random stranger dealt a blow to my self-respect. I've felt better about myself these past few weeks than I have since before Alyssa died. And that's because of you."

His words touch me deeply. I can relate. I know how it feels to be on a seemingly endless quest for fulfillment. I understand the desire that can never be satisfied. The need that comes from deep within and has nothing to do with sex. That need has lessened now that I've reunited with my mother. Now that I understand why she made certain choices. Now that I've forgiven her for abandoning us.

Reaching across the table, I rest my hand on his. "Let's see where these next few months take us. We have plenty to focus on getting ready for the baby."

"And once the baby comes, will you consider my proposal?"

"I'll consider it. As long as you're still interested."

CALVIN INVITES Mom and me to have Thanksgiving with his extended family of aunts, uncles, cousins, and grandparents. They're a boisterous crowd, and they welcome Mom and me with open arms as though we're old friends. They want to know all about the baby. Most feel the need to rub my belly. They're disappointed Calvin and I are not having a gender revealing party.

"I truly don't care what the gender is," I say. "As long as the baby is healthy."

His mother, a tiny woman with Calvin's dark complexion

and amber eyes, leans in close to me. "I like your way of thinking."

They serve dinner at one o'clock. Despite being Italian, the smorgasbord of dishes presented on the sideboard are traditional American Thanksgiving fare. Calvin and I are assigned to eat in the kitchen with the younger generation while Mom joins the grown-ups at the main table in the formal dining room.

Once the dishes are done, the family divides up for a flag football game in the front yard. Mom plays on Calvin's team, and she even scores a touchdown. Afterward, we migrate to the family room by the fire and watch hours of football on television. Around six o'clock, Calvin's mom brings out the leftovers for another round of grazing. Finally, at nine o'clock, Calvin informs me it's time to go.

His mother pulls me aside. "You're a lovely girl, Jolie. Don't break my son's heart."

I smile down at her. "I'm not worried about his heart. I'm worried about mine."

She gives my arm a squeeze. "I know his reputation for being a lady's man. But that's not who he is deep down. For years, I worried he would never get over his sister's death. His pain will always be a part of him, but because of you and the baby, he is finally moving on with his life."

"Thank you for saying that. It means more than you know. Regardless of what happens between us, this child will bind us together forever."

ON CHRISTMAS EVE, Calvin presents me with an engagement ring—a round diamond set between triangular sapphires in an old-fashioned filigree setting. It takes my breath and brings tears to my eyes.

We're alone in the condo. Mom had been here earlier for dinner—an oven roasted beef tenderloin, twice-baked potatoes, and a Caesar salad—and although we begged her to stay and watch reruns of Christmas classics, she insisted she needed to get home because she had a few more presents to wrap. But I think she has a boyfriend. She's been practically giddy these past few weeks. I trust she'll tell me about him when she's ready.

Calvin and I are standing beside the Fraser fir Christmas tree that graces the corner, its tiny white lights reflected in the window. I admire the beautifully wrapped gifts, most of which are courtesy of Mom, piled high at the base.

When I'd told her she went overboard with her shopping, she said, "I have a lot of years to make up for."

My mind wanders as I stand by Calvin patiently holding the box. Jason has been at the forefront of my mind this holiday season. I see him everywhere. In his collection of Christmas ornaments. In cartons of eggnog at the grocery store. In the tacky lights on Monument Avenue. Mom and I went to Hollywood Cemetery last weekend and placed a small cedar wreath on his niche. I still haven't accepted he's gone.

The sound of Calvin clearing his throat brings me back to the present. I smile and look into his eyes as I take the engagement ring out of the box and try it on my finger. It's a perfect fit. "It's lovely, Calvin."

"It belonged to my great grandmother. We can change the setting if you don't like it." He drops to his knees. "Will you marry me, Jolie? You're already the mother of my child. Will you be my wife as well?"

I pull him to his feet. "We agreed not to discuss this until after the baby comes."

He flashes his devilish grin. "Things are going so well between us, I was hoping you'd reconsider."

I'm tempted to say yes. I can no longer deny my feelings. I'm crazy in love with Calvin. But that love is mixed with a fear of failure. I refuse to make this next move until I'm absolutely certain. "I agree things are going well. So why not wait a little longer?"

"But if we get married before the baby comes, we'll be a legitimate family."

I turn my back to him, staring through the window into the dark night. "Why are you suddenly so eager to get married?"

I sense his presence behind me, and I see his reflection in the window, but he doesn't touch me. "So we can be a family. Don't you want that too, Jolie?"

"More than anything. But our marriage needs to be about me and you, not the baby."

Calvin turns me toward him. He tilts his head to the side. I think he's going to kiss me. I hold my breath. I've been waiting for this for so long. I dream of his touch on my skin, his lips on mine. But the man whore has become a monk. Is it because I'm pregnant? Does he find me fat and ugly? Or maybe he's worried he'll hurt the baby.

He kisses the tip of his finger and touches my nose. "Merry Christmas, Jolie. This time next year, we'll be playing Santa for our child. If I have my way about it, we'll be married and living in our own house."

"Here." I hold the ring box out to him, but he refuses to take it.

"You hold on to it. I plan to keep asking you to marry me. Maybe the ring will inspire you to say yes."

And ask he does. Dozens of times during the ensuing months. But he doesn't say the three magic words I desperately need to hear.

Meanwhile, Mom falls head over heels with a handsome doctor who practices with a Concierge Medical Group. Doug Dehart—I call him Dr. Dear Heart—lost his wife to cancer several years ago. They are always together, and I see her less and less. But I'm beyond thrilled for her. She has finally found the true love she deserves.

AT THE BEGINNING OF MARCH, Calvin and I begin preparing the nursery. We clear the furniture out of Jason's room and paint the walls a creamy white. Stacy and Mom host a coed shower for me at Stacy's adorable new house on Maple Street. We receive baby gadgets galore from Calvin's friends, and gender-neutral clothes and towels and blankets from the women.

We take our stash home and set it all up in the nursery. We have everything we need except a crib. I have my heart set on a distressed white crib with clean lines that converts into a toddler bed. The back-ordered crib finally arrives five days before my due date.

Calvin and I spend Saturday afternoon assembling the bed. We're almost finished when a wave of exhaustion overcomes me. "I need to lie down. Do you mind finishing up here?"

Concern crosses his face. "Are you okay?" He's been doting on me since my weekly doctor's appointment when we learned my cervix is dilating.

"I'm fine. Just tired."

I go to my room and stretch out on the bed with a throw blanket covering my swollen belly. A line of thunderstorms is moving through the area, and the sound of driving rain against the window lulls me to sleep.

A feeling of intense pressure against my pelvis wakes me an hour later. When I stand up, water gushes from between my legs. I call out, "Calvin! Come quick! My water just broke."

Seconds later, he appears in the doorway. "I'll get you some dry clothes. Then we should call the doctor."

An excruciating pain rips through my abdomen, and I scream out in pain. "I need to push!"

Moving to the dresser, Calvin opens and closes drawers. "No, you don't, Jolie. This is your first baby. We have hours before it's time to push."

I double over as another contraction tears my body apart. "I'm not kidding, Calvin. This baby is coming right now!"

He whips his phone out of his pocket. "I'll call a rescue squad."

I drop to my knees on the floor. "There's no time. I need to push. I feel the baby's head."

"Let me check you." He helps me lie on my back and yanks off my sodden underwear. With knees bent, I spread my legs wide. "Yep. Baby's crowning."

Another pain, another scream. "What're we gonna do?"

"We're gonna deliver the baby." Calvin gets to his feet. "I'll be right back."

I writhe around on the floor in agony as one contraction after another racks my body. Calvin returns with an armful of supplies. He props bed pillows behind my head, peels back my dress, and places one of the baby's waterproof pads under my bottom.

I grip his arm in terror. "Have you ever delivered a baby before?"

"A few. I was an EMT in high school and college. A surprising number of babies are born in ambulances."

"That was a long time ago." I tighten my grip on his arm. "Call Mom and Dr. Dear Heart."

"They've gone to Charlottesville for the day, remember?"

I groan in response.

"I've got this, Jolie. This is my baby. I won't let you down."

For the next few minutes, he coaches me while I push. Calvin's voice is calm and reassuring, and when the baby makes its appearance into the world, he catches it with a clean towel. Seconds later, the baby's cries fill the room.

I fall back against the pillows, panting. Through the space between my legs, I watch Calvin wiping the baby with a towel. His face is full of tender love. He clamps and cuts the umbilical cord, expertly swaddles the baby in a towel, and hands the bundle to me.

"Meet your son."

I take the baby in my arms and look down at his pinched little face. "He's beautiful."

"I need to deliver the placenta, Jolie. Give me another big push."

I grimace as I bear down one last time. Something wet slides between my legs. Calvin gathers the bloody towels and leaves the room. While he's gone, I examine my child, starting with his ten fingers and toes. He has golden fuzz on his head, the cutest button nose, and rosy lips.

When I look up again, Calvin is standing in the doorway watching us. "An ambulance will be here soon." He comes over and kneels down beside us. "You're amazing, Jolie. I've never loved anyone as much as I love you right now."

"Will you repeat that, please?"

He appears confused. "Which part."

I cross my eyes at him. "You know. The part about you loving me."

Leaning in, he presses his lips against mine. His breath is warm when he whispers, "I love you. Why does that surprise you? I've proposed to you too many times to count."

"And I would've accepted your proposal sooner if you'd said those three magic words."

He falls back on his butt. "You're joking. You mean all this time . . ." His face lights up as though he's suddenly struck with a thought. "So that's what you meant at Christmas when you said our marriage needs to be about me and you, not the baby."

Nodding, I look down at our son. "I want to be more to you than your baby's mother."

He wraps his arms around the baby and me. "You're everything to me, Jolie. I thought you knew that."

"But you never touched me, not one kiss in all these months."

"And you do not know how many cold showers I've taken during that time. I was proving myself to you." He touches his finger to the end of my nose. "I'm marrying you for you. Not for sex. That's not to say I won't be thrilled when the doctor clears you for intimacy."

I wince. "I just delivered a baby. I can't bear the thought of having sex right now."

He reaches on top of the nightstand where I keep the velvet ring box. He opens the box and takes out the ring. "I love you. I love you. I love you. Will you marry me?"

I hold out my left hand. "Damn straight," I say, and he slips the ring on my finger. "I love you too, Calvin Ingram."

"Let me hold him," Calvin says, taking the baby from me. "What're we going to name him?"

We've tossed around names for boys and girls, but we agreed to meet the baby before deciding. "What about Calvin? Don't you want a junior?"

"Not really." He clucks his tongue softly at the baby. "He looks like a Jason to me. What about Jason Hogan Ingram?"

I burst into tears. "Do you mean it, really?"

"I mean it. After all, when God closes a door, he opens a window."

. . .

THANK you for reading *On My Terms*! If you enjoyed this novel, please consider reading my Hope Springs series. Join the unforgettable cast of characters at the historic inn for romance, family drama, and adventure.

You might also like some of my stand alone novels. Be sure to visit my website where you'll find a host of information regarding my inspiration for writing as well as book trailers, reviews, and Pinterest boards from my 20+ other books.

And . . . to find out about my new and upcoming books, be sure to sign up for my newsletter:.

ALSO BY ASHLEY FARLEY

Palmetto Island
Muddy Bottom

Change of Tides

Lowcountry on My Mind

Sail Away

Hope Springs Series
Dream Big, Stella!

Show Me the Way

Mistletoe and Wedding Bells

Matters of the Heart

Stand Alone
Tangled in Ivy

Lies that Bind

Life on Loan

Only One Life

Home for Wounded Hearts

Nell and Lady

Sweet Tea Tuesdays

Saving Ben

Sweeney Sisters Series
Saturdays at Sweeney's

Tangle of Strings

Boots and Bedlam

Lowcountry Stranger

Her Sister's Shoes

Magnolia Series

Beyond the Garden

Magnolia Nights

Scottie's Adventures

Breaking the Story

Merry Mary

ACKNOWLEDGMENTS

I'm grateful to many people for helping make this novel possible. Foremost, to my editor, Patricia Peters, for her patience and advice and for making my work stronger without changing my voice. A great big heartfelt thank-you to my trusted beta readers —Alison Fauls, Anne Wolters, Laura Glenn, Jan Klein, Lisa Hudson, Lori Walton, Kathy Sinclair, and Jenelle Rodenbaugh. A special thank you to my behind-the-scenes, go-to girl, Kate Rock, for all the many things you do to manage my social media so effectively.

I am blessed to have many supportive people in my life who offer the encouragement I need to continue the pursuit of my writing career. I owe an enormous debt of gratitude to my advanced review team, the lovely ladies of Georgia's Porch, for their enthusiasm for and commitment to my work. To Leslie Rising at Levy's for being my local bookshop. Love and thanks to my family—my mother, Joanne; my husband, Ted; and my amazing kiddos, Cameron and Ned.

Most of all, I'm grateful to my wonderful readers for their love of women's fiction. I love hearing from you. Feel free to shoot me an email at ashleyhfarley@gmail.com or stop by my website at ashleyfarley.com for more information about my characters and upcoming releases. Don't forget to sign up for my newsletter. Your subscription will grant you exclusive content, sneak previews, and special giveaways.

ABOUT THE AUTHOR

Ashley Farley writes books about women for women. Her characters are mothers, daughters, sisters, and wives facing real-life issues. Her bestselling Sweeney Sisters series has touched the lives of many.

Ashley is a wife and mother of two young adult children. While she's lived in Richmond, Virginia for the past 25 years, a piece of her heart remains in the salty marshes of the South Carolina Lowcountry, where she still calls home. Through the eyes of her characters, she captures the moss-draped trees, delectable cuisine, and kindhearted folk with lazy drawls that make the area so unique.

Ashley loves to hear from her readers. Visit Ashley's Website @ashleyfarley.com

Get free exclusive content by signing up for her newsletter @ ashleyfarley.com/newsletter-signup/

facebook.com/ashleywfarley

twitter.com/AshleyWFarley

instagram.com/ashleyfarleyauthor

Ingram Content Group UK Ltd.
Milton Keynes UK
UKHW011050260323
419169UK00006B/717